RENDERED

Book 1 in the Irrevocable Series

Samantha Jacobey

ISBN: **0692420797**
ISBN-13: **978-0692420799**

RENDERED

Book 1 in the Irrevocable Series

Samantha Jacobey

Lavish Publishing, LLC ~ Houston

Copyright

First Edition

Book 1 of Irrevocable Series

All Rights Reserved

Published in the United States by Lavish Publishing, LLC, Houston

Cover Design by: Nicolene Lorette Design

Cover Images: Shutterstock

Paperback ISBN

ISBN 10: 0692420797

ISBN 13: 978-0692420799

www.LavishPublishing.com

.

TABLE OF CONTENTS

For my mother, Linda. Without her, much of this tale could not, or would not, have been written. Thank you for our family, which has taught me what crazy really means…

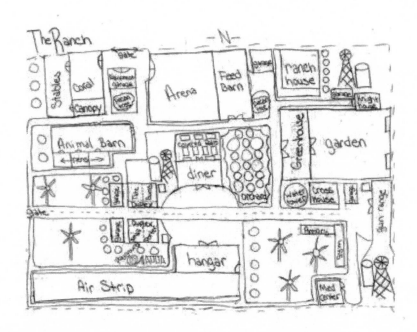

PROLOGUE

"I just can't believe it," Pamela smiled across the table at her husband, reaching for him affectionately.

"You can't?" Lewis Dewitt grinned, entwining his fingers with hers, "Twenty years and you still take my breath away." Rubbing the back of her hand with a restless thumb, his thoughts grew distant, filled with the memory of the day they met. His voice softened, "Did you ever think we would make it this far?"

"Not a chance," she gave him a quick squeeze before withdrawing her digits, and the waiter placed their steaming plates before them. "Wow, this looks delicious." Using her fork, she inspected the vegetables and began cutting her steak with the oversized knife.

"You didn't think we were made for each other?" he quibbled, adjusting his napkin and preparing to devour his own.

"Of course not," she flicked her soft blue eyes at him,

"But you were so persistent. At least we had the sense to finish college before we married, and then waited three more years before Bailey was born."

"Right," he nodded between bites, "Our baby girl is growing up, Pam. She'll be a senior next year, and then she's off to college. We should do everything we can to spend time with her before she goes."

His wife laughed gently at the suggestion. "She doesn't really have time for us any more, honey. You know with all those Advanced Placement Courses, and cheerleading. God forbid she gets a boyfriend." She inhaled a long breath through her nose, exhaling it through a relaxed jaw. "I try not to think about it, and I take what time I can get."

"Yes," he agreed quickly, sorry he had put a damper on the mood with his observation. "Don't worry, she'll still have time for us. And maybe she'll follow our lead, and wait until she's old enough to appreciate certain things before she starts getting involved in any relationships. You know, she has a good head on her shoulders. Takes after you."

His wife grinned at the compliment, "She takes after both of us. It's those boys that are going to be trouble. I swear, if I had known what a handful they would be, I might have passed on the fertility doctor!"

"Oh, stop it," Lewis chided, "You love those boys, hot mess and all. Besides, they're half grown as well, and then it'll be the two of us. About the time that Bailey starts to give us some grandkids to dote over, I should think."

Pamela blinked at him for a moment. "You just gave me the craziest swarm of butterflies! I don't even want to *think* about grand babies yet, much less about the boys growing up." It had been a long road with Jase and Jess, and although they were nine years old, it was hard not to think of them as small and delicate, the way they had started out in life.

The skin around Lewis' brown orbs crinkled with his smile, "It's ok, babe. We've got twenty years in tonight, and what... another forty to go?"

"You bet we do," she raised her glass of wine as a toast, "To the man I wasn't supposed to marry, and thank God every day that I did. May we do this again in another twenty years!" Her mate raised his own crystal, allowing them to touch with a soft tinkle before he swallowed the delicious libation and returned it to the fine linen cloth that covered the table.

IN THE BEGINNING

Bailey lay staring at the ceiling, listening intently. A moment later, she heard the loud banging again, followed by the ring of the doorbell in a string of peals. *What the hell?* Rolling over enough to see her clock, she noted the time; one-thirty-six. Watching it, the last number flicked to a seven, while the ruckus continued, and she decided maybe her parents couldn't hear the racket.

"Hard to believe that," she grumbled to herself. Sliding out of the bed, she pulled on her favorite fluffy housecoat and fumbled her way into the hall. Making her way down the stairs, she stretched and yawned, wrapping the gown more tightly before she opened the wide wooden covering, "Do you have any idea what time it is?" she shrieked before catching her breath at the sight of the men before her.

"As a matter of fact, we do," the officer spoke through pursed lips, "Is this the Dewitt residence?"

"Yes, it is," Bailey could feel her heart in her throat, "My parents must not have heard you. Give me a minute, and I'll get them."

"That won't be necessary," the other uniformed visitor, Olsen by his name tag, offered quickly, "May we come in?"

A sick feeling of mild panic crept up her spine as she pushed at her long auburn hair. "Sure, this way," she indicated the sitting room to her left. Her mind turning, she debated whether or not the two men were actually cops, or if she had let a pair of murderers into her home.

Removing his hat, Officer Olsen ran his fingers through his dark curls, "When was the last time you saw your parents, Miss Dewitt?"

"Last night," she replied coolly, curling her toes nervously inside her soft slippers. "It was their anniversary, and I watched the boys so they could go out." *Surely they don't suspect my parents of anything!* She mentally struggled to get a grip on her scattered thoughts. *And I'm sure they don't interrogate people in the middle of the night in their bath robe, either.*

Lifting a finger to graze the edge of a silver photo frame, he nodded, "I'm sorry ma'am, but we're here to inform you of an accident. A few minutes before midnight, a semi took out a black BMW over on Clayton Hill. Crossed the line in a curve and both the truck and the car tumbled to the bottom of the canyon. I truly am sorry."

The girl stared at him with wide green eyes, her face like fine porcelain, frozen for an instant before it cracked. "That can't be," she stammered, "My parents are here. The boys and I went to bed hours ago, and my parents came home. I'll show you!" she called over her shoulder, making a dash for the stair case.

Reaching the second floor landing, "Mom!" her voice cried loudly, and her hands shook as she flung open the master suite's door, "Dad!" Inside the room, she stopped short, her robe hanging open and allowing the cool air to wash over her body. Before her, the bed lay empty, and hadn't been touched.

Shaking her head, hot tears began to streak down her face, "NO, NO, this isn't right!" Hearing the floor creak, she spun around to face the two men, who had followed closely behind her.

Raising a hand to grasp her shoulder, Olsen gave her a squeeze, "We need to call someone, a relative or friend of the family, who can come over."

Her fingers trembling, she covered her face, "Yes," she sobbed her agreement, "I'll call my grandmother. She'll know what to do."

Her hand trailing the banister on the way down, Bailey made her way to her parents' home office, to the right of the entrance. Inside her mother's desk, she would find the small brown address book that contained all the important information for both clients and family; her mother's backup in case anything ever happened to her cellphone.

Standing in the foyer, the two men allowed the girl to make the call, her voice quavering while she asked the woman to come over quickly. At being questioned, the girl gave a simple and non-committal reply, "There's been an accident, Nanna. We need you here, as quickly as you can come."

Unable to bring herself to say more, Bailey pushed the button to end the call. She returned the house phone to the little pedestal and blinked at the glowing light that indicated it had been seated correctly.

Hovering by the front entrance, Olsen watched the girl adjust her robe and reach for tissues. She kept her back to him, her shoulders rounded and hunched. After a moment, he called out softly, "We should move to the other room. We can sit in the living area so we can hear the door, and wait."

Moving to comply, Bailey made her way across the hall, her slippers sliding smoothly on the polished hard wood. Perched on the front edge of the sofa, she sat up straight, her eyes darting around at the formal furnishings. Her heart pounded anxiously against her ribs, and her palms tingled. She felt odd, and recalled, *I've never sat on this couch before.*

The girl rocked slightly, back and forth, considering her mother's rules and procedures. The children were not permitted in the front living room; or pretty much anywhere in the house for that matter. A play room had been constructed on the back side, off of the kitchen, when the boys were born. That was theirs; that and their bedrooms. *Everything else is off limits.*

Staring at the large clock above the fireplace, she watched the minutes tick by. Her tears had stopped, and aside from the occasional sniffle, it was impossible to tell she had ever been upset. Squeezing the tissue in her palm, she waited, unsure how she would break the news to her mother's mother. Fortunately, she wouldn't have to.

When the bell sounded, Officer Olsen moved to allow the elderly woman inside, and explained the situation to her. Bailey could hear the commotion as her grandmother bellowed, an odd sound really, as they were not a family accustomed to such displays of emotion.

Standing, Bailey held out her arms, relieved that someone else was there. Someone besides the two stiff policemen, who could do nothing but bear bad news. *Nanna will fix this,* she reassured herself as she clung to the frail body; *she'll know what to do.*

It isn't fair, Bailey thought to herself while sitting in the bay window of the breakfast nook the day after her parents' funeral. Blinking back tears, she reached up to trace a drop of moisture while it ran down the pane. It had been raining almost non-stop since the morning the police had brought their dark tidings. Exhaling a deep sigh, she pulled her knees up to lean on.

"Why can't we stay here?" she demanded bitterly, no longer afraid of upsetting her grandmother. "If you don't want to let us live with you and Gramps?"

"Because, you're only sixteen years old," her grandmother countered firmly.

The girl didn't take her eyes off of the glass, and the garden beyond. *It'll be blooming in a few weeks,* she pouted slightly. "This is our home, Nanna. And I'll be seventeen in two months." She could hear the disgruntled noise behind her, and tried a different track, "Either way, you should let us go and live with you, if we can't live here anymore," she implored. "Please."

"In the retirement community?" her grandmother quipped. "Our little apartment only has two bedrooms and you know this. Besides, we've done our part, raising your mother and her brother. It's our time to rest and enjoy our old age."

Old age, Bailey scoffed, then dropped her legs and twisted on the seat, watching the grey hair move about in their kitchen. Her eyes narrowed at the way her uncle was referred to as *your mother's brother* regularly. "You don't even like Uncle Peter. No one does. Why would you make us go and live with him?"

"Because your father didn't have any relatives even remotely able to take you; Peter is young, he has a good job, and he can support you."

"And his wife died and he doesn't have any kids of his own," Bailey insisted, "Don't you think he's going to be unhappy if you force us on him? Besides, he's older than mom was, and therefore *not* young."

Sipping from her ceramic mug, the elderly woman remained calm, a small smile teasing her lips, "Such is life, my child."

Hearing the doorbell at the front of the house, Bailey cringed. The boys were the first ones there, chattering loudly at the arrival of their favorite, and only, uncle.

She wasn't sure what she had expected, having not seen her relative in over a decade, but whatever it had been, this wasn't it. Her jaw hanging open slightly, she managed to clamp it shut as the tall sandy-haired man made his way into the room, the twins badgering him every step of the way.

"Well, if it isn't little Bailey, looking all grown up!" He smiled brightly at her, while she ignored the comment and turned back to the rain with another sigh, curling her legs beneath her.

Peter Mason was a slender man, a few years over fifty, with shaggy curls that held only the slightest hint of grey. An ex-marine, he was still in excellent health, with toned muscles and flat abs beneath his shirt and leather jacket. "I missed you the last time I was here," he called out to her, pouring himself a cup of coffee, "Something about summer camp."

"That was ages ago," the girl replied without moving.

"I see the boys remember you."

He laughed at her observation, shooing the pair out of the room with the promise of coming up stairs shortly. Making an excuse, his mother followed them, leaving uncle and niece to get reacquainted.

"No, they really don't," he replied, "They were only two last time I was here, but that's ok. At least they're excited." He took a seat at the table, facing the girl, "I really am sorry, Bailey. I know things aren't working out the way you would've liked."

She swung her legs off the bench to sit up straight and glare at him. "Not working out? How could my parents dying suddenly possibly be anything less than perfect?" she demanded coldly.

Pete's jaw dropped slightly, rocking side to side, "You get that from your mother, you know. It's what made her such a damn good attorney."

"What?" the girl practically screamed.

"Your tough as nails attitude," he smiled genuinely. "When we get back to Texas and settled in, you an' me are gonna be great friends. I can tell." He sipped his brew calmly, waiting to see if she would bite.

Blowing out a disgusted breath, the girl didn't engage. Instead, she stood and stomped noisily out of the room and up the stairs. Taking care to make as much racket as possible, she punctuated the move by slamming her bedroom door behind her.

I'm not going to Texas, she promised herself silently. Flinging her body across the bed, she managed to hide in her private space until it had grown dark outside, and she was no longer able to ignore the angry rumble in her gut.

Making her way back down to the kitchen, she discovered the rest of her family, such as it was, gathered at the table and eating pizza. Looking around, she sniffed noisily, then poured herself a glass of soda. "Where's Nanna?" she finally huffed, grabbing a paper plate.

"She went home," Jess eagerly volunteered.

Shifting her glare to her uncle, Bailey could feel the flush rising in her neck. "Just like that?"

"Just like that," Pete shook his head slightly, biting off of a fresh slice. "We'll pack each of you a suitcase either tonight or in the morning. Our plane leaves O'Hare at eleven o'clock, so there won't be any need to rush."

"I'm not going."

Her brothers stared at her, dumbfounded by her response, but her uncle remained cool. "We'll talk about that in a bit. After dinner."

Refusing to let it go, she countered, "What about all our stuff?" She waved her hands to indicate their belongings, "You expect us to go off and live with you with only a suitcase full of clothes?"

"Your grandmother has arranged for someone to pack your rooms. All of your personal items will be sent to us."

"And what about everything else?" she demanded loudly.

"It's up to Louise to decide," he continued to chew. "Look, Bailey, you grew up in this family the same as I did. I'm sure by now you've figured out that Louise Mason runs the show, and whatever she says goes."

"And what's that supposed to mean?"

"It means we're in this together, you an' me," Pete cut his eyes over at the girl, "An' we're gonna make the best of it." Glancing back at the boys, he hoped everything they did wouldn't be such a hassle; but if she were like every other woman in the Mason clan, he knew that would be wishful thinking.

A WHOLE NEW WORLD

Bailey lay in her bed, blinking at the suitcase she had reluctantly packed the night before. Watching the light slowly surround it and bring it out of the shadows, she thought about the argument she had given her uncle over her moving to Texas to live with him. In the end, he had won, mainly because she realized she was going, one way or another, and if she wanted a say in her wardrobe when she got there, she had better do the honors.

Sliding out of bed, she slunk over to her computer and switched it on. Her parents had purchased it for her the year before, when she entered high school, but she rarely used it, preferring her phone for keeping in touch with her mass of friends. Leaning on her elbow, palm mashing against her cheek, she watched the screen go from black to blue, and her icons began popping into place.

What the hell am I going to tell them? She had many *friends* on her page, and typically made several posts a day. Since her parents died, she had only made two, and they were brief at best. However, the time had come for her to make the announcement; she wouldn't be returning to school after all.

Typing the text into the box, a single tear slipped from her eye and rolled down her cheek. Wiping it away in frustration, her gaze darted over to her memo board on the wall next to her desk. Covered with pictures of her and her friends, it held images of her adventures as a cheerleader, and all of the other clubs and organizations that she belonged to.

Drawing a ragged breath, she reached for a tissue, her mind still caught up in the memory of her social life. *Mom saw to it that I was able to do whatever I wanted. She would be heartbroken if she knew they were making me leave it all behind.* Turning her attention back to the wide screen, she began to compose her message.

Using agile fingers, Bailey typed out a status update: *As many of you know, we have suffered a tragedy at our house, and I will not be returning to Lincoln. I will miss you all dearly, and keep in touch.* Clicking the blue post button, she released a heavy sigh and slumped back in the seat.

Well, that wasn't so hard. She could imagine how upset her friends would be to learn of her situation, and of her forced move to Texas. She felt glad she had refrained from posting every grimy detail, as many of the girls she knew would have done. *But that wouldn't be proper. Mom taught me that.*

As a wealthy attorney, sharing a practice with her husband, Pamela Dewitt had taken great care in the grooming of their daughter and sons. The family held a high status in the mid-sized town, and having any dirty laundry aired publicly was a huge no-no. Things were always kept in order, with children that behaved as they were expected.

Glancing at the photos once more, the girl made it to her feet and began the process of getting dressed. Then, a random thought entered her mind, and she sat back on the edge of her chair. Navigating to Google, she typed in *Midland, Texas*, to find out what she could about their destination.

A few clicks later, she wanted to throw the keyboard onto the floor in disgust. *It's hot, it's dry, and it's in the middle of nowhere,* she grimaced. On her feet again, she shut down the machine and finished gathering her things while fuming in a loud whisper.

Downstairs, she pulled her suitcase up next to the door, her head popping up when she recognized her grandfather's laugh. "Gramps!" she called, bouncing towards the kitchen. Throwing her arms around his neck, she was prepared to make one last attempt, "Please don't make us move to Texas. Or, let the boys go with Uncle Pete, and I can stay with you!" Perching on his lap, she clung to him for effect.

His green eyes that matched her own stared at her

vacantly for a moment, "What? You mean you would let those two go off without you? You're their big sister, Bailey-girl, you're supposed to be looking out for them. Now how're you gonna do that if you stay here?"

Slowly removing herself from his arms, she could feel the hopelessness creeping over her. "So, you think I should go with them, too?"

"That's right, you belong together. I'm really disappointed you didn't see this for yourself. We always take care of our own; with your mom and dad gone, your little brothers are your responsibility." His brow crinkled when he spoke, and Bailey hung her head slightly at his rebuke.

"I'm sorry, Gramps. I just thought Uncle Peter would be good enough, and they don't really need me." Moving away from him, she took out a bowl for cereal, noticing for the first time her brothers seated at the table, observing in silence.

"You don't wanna go with us?" one of the twins asked in a dejected voice, his eyes wide with emotion.

Tilting her head to take in his small, round face, the girl could see his hurt, easy to read in his wide brown eyes. "It's ok, Jase, I'm going with you. And I'm going to look out for you, too. I promise."

The boy's chin lifted immediately, and a smile exposed the gap where his new front teeth had begun to poke through the gums. Returning her gaze to her breakfast, she stifled the urge to sigh loudly. *I don't want to go,* she rationalized, *but keeping up the argument isn't helping, and they have sidestepped me at every turn. I need a different plan.*

Two hours later, the group arrived at the airport. Making it through security easily enough, Bailey and Peter took seats next to one another in the gate area, while the boys pressed themselves against the wide section of glass to watch the planes.

Removing her phone from her pocket, Bailey opened her Facebook app and began to skim through her newsfeed. Normally, she would have done this several times a day, but since the accident, it didn't feel right. Something about seeing everyone's happy news and *liking* their posts made her feel even more lost than she already did.

Shifting in his seat so that he could observe her actions, Pete kept one eye on her, and the other on the boys. After a good fifteen minutes of silence, he leaned a little closer to her, "You know, it's ok to cry."

Her thumb frozen over the device, she cut her eyes over at him before lifting her face, "I don't need advice from you."

Smiling at her show of bravado, he quipped, "Just trying to help. I know this isn't what you wanted, but we can still be friends."

"No, thanks," she pressed the button to darken the screen and slipped the android into her pocket. Standing abruptly, she made her way over to the boys and took a seat on the ledge next to them. "Anything good out there?"

"It's not good," Jess squealed, "It's AWESOME!"

His sister's lips hinted at a grin at his excitement. Aware that neither of them had been on a plane before, she felt they were entitled. "That's cool, sweet pea. You enjoy the planes."

Glancing around at the rest of the passengers in waiting, she longed to be somewhere else, preferably alone. Her gaze landing on her uncle, she noticed he stared at them... or was it her that he watched so intently?

Tossing her crimson highlights, she looked away, leaning on her hand and observing him out of the corner of her eye. She could see the odd, half smile that he wore, making her even more uncomfortable. *What was it everyone always said about Uncle Peter?* She struggled to recall, but it had been years since anyone in her family had spoken of him at all.

Shifting, she turned to glare at him, giving him the evil eye. This only caused him to show his perfect white teeth in a wide grin. *Damn him.* The fact that he didn't look away after being caught gave her an ominous feeling in the pit of her stomach. *My parents didn't like him... I wish I could remember why.*

Their plane touched down at Midland International Airport at two-thirty that afternoon. Exiting the tunnel and surveying the interior, Bailey laughed out loud,

"How the hell does this dinky little place warrant the name *International*? It's only got five gates, for Christ's sake!"

Peter walked beside her calmly, choosing to ignore her negativity, "Did you boys enjoy your first flight?"

"YES!" they agreed simultaneously, dodging through the crowd.

Leaving the upper deck and making their way over to the baggage claim, the girl continued to point out flaws in their new surroundings, "Have you ever seen so many stupid hats?"

"That's enough!" her new guardian demanded in a clipped tone. "These people are your new neighbors and friends, an' they won' take kindly to that attitude."

She cut her green eyes over, squinting in defiance, but held her tongue.

Catching the handle of the bags, Peter pulled them off the conveyer one by one. Making sure each of the boys had their handles extended properly, they were ready to wheel their luggage out behind them. He then directed them into the covered parking, where what appeared to be a brand new SUV awaited them.

The boys scurried into the back seat right away, eager to mess with the video player that hung from the roof. To their delight, a selection of movies filled a small storage box. Giving the front passenger door a heavy slam, Bailey wrinkled her nose; *that's a hell of a bribe,* she mentally noted. Aloud, she queried, "Did you just get this thing?"

"What thing?" her uncle replied, sliding behind the wheel.

"This car," she grimaced, opening the glove box, which was immaculate; and empty.

"Yeah," he started the engine and pulled out of the space, "I figured I would need a family vehicle if I were going to be carting you three around, so I picked it up before I left." He didn't look at her, and kept his eyes on the road when they exited the pay terminal, again giving the girl an odd feeling in her gut.

Gazing out the window, she noted the sparse number of buildings surrounding the airport; *this place really is in the middle of nowhere.* About fifteen minutes later, they found civilization, and soon arrived at the apartment that would be their new home.

Lugging their suitcases up the stairs, they made their way inside to the living room, which had been furnished with a tan colored sectional sofa. In the far wall, she could see a narrow window centered above the oversized couch, which allowed whoever was in the kitchen to see out into the front room. To the right of that, a small dining table filled a wide open alcove, a sliding glass door behind the vertical blinds, which led to the tiny balcony.

Moving further in, she looked to her right, and noticed that the sectional formed a half-wall of sorts, so that sitting on it meant the kitchen and dining were to your back. Everything in the house seemed to face the cherry-wood entertainment center that stood to the right of the front door as you entered, a small blind-covered window sandwiched between them. The large wooden cabinet contained a hefty flat screen television, a blue-ray machine, and two different gaming systems, with two full shelves of movies and games.

Eyeballing her uncle warily, Bailey bit her lip to keep from asking. She could tell the furnishings were brand new, same as the Suburban he drove. *Why get new stuff just for us?* It bothered her that he would do so, and she could feel her distrust of the man who was appointed as their guardian growing by the minute. Instead she said simply, "Which way to our rooms?"

"Back here," Peter grabbed a boy's bag in each hand and hauled them down the hall, which exited the living area to the left. Arriving at the first door on the right, he carried them in and put them on the floor next to the chest of drawers. On the far right wall stood a new set of bunk beds, complete with comforters in the boys' favorite cartoon characters.

Staring at the furnishings, complete with pictures on the walls and a desk for them to share, her anger began to boil. "How do you know so much about them?" she demanded, while observing that the bathroom lay across the hall from their door and the entire apartment smelled like a furniture store.

"Huh," the man grunted, "I asked. Your room is this

way," he indicated the next room down on the right side of the hall, which happened to be the end. "Yours isn't decorated. I thought I'd let you do that for yourself." His voice sounded tired, and he didn't bother to go in. Instead he turned his back and entered the door that faced hers. That being his quarters, he closed the door behind him, leaving the kids to unpack their things and settle in.

BLACK AND WHITE

Bailey reluctantly emptied her suitcase, placing her clothes into the drawers of the small chest or hanging them in the closet. Looking around, her room seemed barren. Mentally starting her shopping list, she would be sure to pick up an ironing board as soon as possible; *being in a new town is no excuse to turn into a slouch.*

While making her plans, she noted that Peter came out of his room, closing the door behind him, and she heard him ask the boys if they could put their own clothes away. *Of course they can,* she scoffed mentally. *Man, he sure doesn't know anything about kids.* Peeking down the narrow passage, she smiled faintly at their eagerness to divide up their new personal space, while the head of the household exited via the front door without so much as a word to her.

As soon as he left, Bailey felt gripped with the urge to explore the rest of the apartment. *I don't want to get caught though, so I need to make this quick.* Scooting across the hall, she entered his room to discover that it held a new matching bedroom suite, complete with a king-sized bed. Opening a few drawers, she found that the top one contained a handful of briefs and six pairs of socks, but the rest were empty.

Swinging around to the closet, she counted two pairs of jeans, two pairs of dress slacks, and ten shirts at most. *There's no way he makes do with such a small amount of clothing.* She hadn't decided what she suspected the man of, but each new discovery only caused her uneasy feeling to grow.

After a quick glance towards the front door, she felt safe to head to the kitchen, where she opened the fridge to find a few bottles of water. *No condiments. What kind of person doesn't even have mustard and ketchup in their house?* Opening a few cabinets, she found a few canned goods, but the freezer was barren.

Confident she was on to something, she knelt down to check under the sink. With a quick peek, she discovered a sponge, still in the cellophane, along with a small bottle of dish soap, and an unopened box of trash bags. *He definitely doesn't live here. All new, as if he bought it either for show, or literally on his way out of town to pick us up.*

Deciding to hang on to her discoveries until they were relevant to disclose, she made her way over to have a look around outside. Stepping out onto the balcony, the girl froze.

Pete stood at the stairs, leaning on the support post with his back to her. "Yeah, I know, but no, it's ok. I'll bring them out as soon as I'm able. An' don't worry about the girl, I'll figure…" he stopped in mid-sentence, allowing the phone to drift away from his ear when he realized he wasn't alone. "You need something?" he addressed her curtly.

"No, I was… just going to have a look around," she stammered.

"Well, don't," he wafted a hand at her to shoo her back inside, "We'll come out later an' I'll show you the sights." When she didn't budge, he snapped the phone shut, without even a goodbye to the other end. "What's the matter, are you hungry already?"

"Of course," she leapt at the excuse, "It's almost dinner time back home."

"This is home," he countered smoothly, pushing past her to check on the boys, "Hey guys, you ready for some grub?" His voice had lifted when he spoke to them, and they came bounding out of their room to meet him.

"Are all those toys and stuff for us?" Jess asked with obvious excitement.

"Yup, they sure are!" Pete grinned, "An' I'm gonna get you two a computer to share this weekend. How would you like that?"

"I don't think they're old enough for that," Bailey bit her words angrily, furious at his obvious attempt to buy her younger siblings' affections with all the toys and gadgets.

"Well, since I'm the grown up here, an' I say they can have one, I guess I win." He didn't look at her as he spoke, and she found his dismissal of her and her opinion more than frustrating.

Scowling, Bailey helped gather the boys, and they made their way down to the car. True to his word, Peter pointed out the highlights of their apartment complex, including where the office was located, as well as the laundromat, which earned him a disgusted glare. Pulling out onto the street, they traveled down the block to a small restaurant and made their way through the entrance.

Inside the crowded eatery, they were forced to sit on a bench and wait twenty minutes for a table. "Why did we come here?" she demanded crossly under her breath.

"Because the food is good, and it's convenient," her uncle shot back.

"Well, why couldn't we find some place we don't have to wait?"

"There is no such place," his voice dropped, still disturbed by her attitude. "Midland is booming, and there's far more people here than facilities. We take what we can get, an' we don't complain. There are long lines, waits, an' traffic everywhere we go."

"Great," the girl sighed, casting her eyes over the crowd, many of whom were standing in the congested foyer. *Well, at least we're sitting,* she consoled herself while continuing to frown.

A few minutes later, they were shown to a table, and the boys eagerly unwrapped their crayons to work on their masterpieces. Grinning at the youngsters, Bailey inquired, "You guys want chicken strips tonight?"

Jase and Jess agreed in unison, and Bailey chose a steak with a baked potato and salad. Pulling out her phone, she skimmed through her news feed to discover that a few hundred people had liked and commented on her final post. Darkening her device, she emitted a large sigh; *man this sucks. I have to find a way to get home.*

Eating her dinner in silence, she peered around at their quaint surroundings. Eventually, she allowed herself to ponder what her friends were doing at the moment, her mood descending further when her mind turned to what her evening would have held in store if she hadn't been dragged away from her normal life.

Peter ate in near silence, only occasionally asking the boys a question or answering one of theirs. He noted the two of them were deeply attached, and got along extremely well. He grinned while watching them, happy they were taking all the changes in stride. The girl on the other hand, appeared sullen, and seldom had anything positive to say.

Realizing he had to return to work the following morning, and the kids had school, he chose to keep their outing short. Only making a quick stop at the grocery store before heading back to the apartment, he wanted to ensure everyone would get a good night of sleep in their new home. In the end, he wasn't sure what he would do about the auburn-haired girl and her attitude, but he knew he needed to figure it out quick. *Otherwise, I'll have to decide how I'm gonna get rid of her.*

PROM QUEEN

Rising early after a fitful sleep, Bailey chose her attire for her first day at school. *A new place and new kids.* She thought she should be nervous, but had a dull ache in her chest instead; and the longing to go home. She had been nominated for prom queen, which would be taking place the weekend coming up. She exhaled loudly at the realization she would miss it.

"Why did they have to die?" she whispered under her breath; *it has ruined everything.* She knew she wouldn't win; senior girls always did, but it was still her moment to shine, and it was gone.

Pulling on her jeans and shirt, she moved to the bathroom, where she put on her makeup and styled her long tresses. Bailey firmly put her dark thoughts aside while she worked. *I need to make a few friends here, and carrying around all that baggage isn't going to help that happen.* Besides, thinking about losing her parents was painful, and she would do whatever it took to avoid it.

Hearing sounds outside the door, the girl finished her primping, then practiced smiling into the mirror. Choosing the one she liked the best, she made sure she could reach the expression easily, and began rehearsing her story. Making her way to the kitchen, the eggs and bacon her uncle had prepared smelled delicious, and she sneered at the idea that the role of maid suited him.

"Do I need to wake the boys?" she inquired sedately.

"Not yet," Pete replied, filling their plates. "I'll call them in a few minutes." Replacing the skillet on the stove, he gathered some papers and took his seat in front of the steaming meal. "Let's get you squared away first, then I can deal with them."

Glancing over at the stack, "What's all this?" She could tell one of the items was a map, but its purpose, so far, was unclear.

"Well, you don't have a vehicle, and since everything is spread out, you're gonna need a way to get around," he replied calmly, causing the girl's jaw to drop.

"Mom or dad took me everywhere," her voice squeaked slightly; *I hadn't thought of that.*

"Yeah, well, as there's only one o' me an' I work all day; you'll be taking the bus," he pushed the map towards her as he spoke, ignoring her gaping expression. "This's the layout of the routes, an' I marked the area where you're allowed to go. All o' this stuff," he dragged his fingers over portions that had been shaded with a pencil, "Is a no fly zone. You can go to school, and you can be here, at the apartment. This's the mall," he thumped the page, "An' this's Wal-Mart."

"Wal-Mart?" she scoffed. "Who the hell shops at *Wal-Mart*?"

Cutting his eyes up to glare at her without raising his chin, he clipped, "From now on, you do." Folding his hands in front of his face, he tapped his extended index fingers against his lips, resisting the urge to belittle her. "I know your mother had her way of doing things, but she's gone. You'll find that I'm a lot simpler t' live with. A lot less complicated. No maids, no entertaining; just ordinary."

The girl stared at him, turning her fork over her plate. Clenching her teeth, she could feel the hot flush rising in her neck, "What's wrong with the way my *mother* did things?" she demanded curtly, emphasizing the word mother loudly.

"Not a thing," Peter lifted his cup to sip the warm brew. Leaning back in his chair, he allowed the pause to grow long, watching the fire in the girl's green eyes. "You're a lot like her. Uptight. You should learn to relax more. Enjoy your life, Bailey." Rising, he left her to look over the materials while he got the boys up and ready to leave.

Reaching over with an extended finger, the girl pushed the map to the side, finding a few pieces of paper and a card with *Bus Pass* in bold letters across it. Lifting it to inspect it more closely, she discovered she could use it for an unlimited number of rides, valid for the entire month.

"I guess I'll get a new one when I need it?" she asked, her voice considerably quieter when he rejoined her.

"Yeah," he flopped into his seat, "I'll get you a new one on the first. It'll do to finish out this year an' we can discuss your transportation for next year after you've settled in." He smiled at her, noticing the small pout that she wore. "You'll be ok. The bus is perfectly safe. Stick to the places I gave you, an' you'll be fine."

The boys joined them at that moment, and Bailey quickly downed the rest of her breakfast while they ate cereal and milk. Rinsing her plate and fork, she loaded them into the dishwasher and went to brush her teeth, a little forlorn at the sound of her brothers' laughter; *they don't even seem to care that mom and dad are gone.*

The small party arrived at the elementary school a short time later, where registering the boys only took a few minutes. Bailey and her uncle walked them to their class, their excitement easy to see as they chattered to one another and pointed out their new surroundings.

Hanging back while her uncle introduced the boys to their teacher, she speculated the fact that they had each other made it seem so easy for them. *Me, on the other hand,* she rolled her eyes with a sigh; *I'm on my own.*

Returning to the Suburban a few minutes later, the silence hung heavily between them. During the ride the few blocks to the high school, Bailey gasped, "What about the boys, if you have to work? How're they getting home?"

Peter grinned at her sudden concern for someone other than herself, and collected his thoughts a moment before he responded. "They're going to a daycare after school. They'll be picked up, an' I'll get them on my way home in the evening. There's food at the house, an' since you'll be arriving first, I'd appreciate it if you'd start dinner for us around five o'clock."

Her mouth hung open slightly, "And what makes you think I can cook?"

"There's some frozen dinners in the freezer from our shopping last night. Just follow the directions on the box. You can read, can't you?" he suggested, baring his perfect white teeth as if to mock her.

"Yes, I can read," she turned back to the window, noting the size of the building and the amount of traffic surrounding her new campus. "How many kids are here?"

"I think it's two or three thousand," he replied. "There's two high schools, and they're both full. Like I said, the town's booming right now, so there's not enough places to live, and everywhere you go, it's crowded."

"You found a place to live," she turned to watch his reaction to her prodding.

"Yeah," he pursed his lips, "My company pulled some strings to get the apartment for me so you guys would have a place to stay."

She frowned at his simple and brief response, but let it go for the time being.

Parking in a visitor's spot, the pair climbed out of the vehicle and crossed the busy street. "I see the bus stop down there," Peter pointed to the left side of the building. "That's where you'll catch the bus this afternoon. You'll have to swipe your pass, so make sure you don't lose it, or you're stuck."

Bailey grunted with a nod, still angry that she was going to be taking public transportation. "I won't lose it. I'm not stupid," she spit, earning her a dark glance at the front doors.

Inside, her schedule waited for her, as her records had been faxed from her previous school. "Do I need to walk you to class?" her guardian teased, his eyes darting around the bustling breezeway outside the office.

"God, no! I don't need a babysitter," Bailey turned her back on him and walked away, leaving him standing alone in the sea of bodies.

Making it through her day, Bailey used her smile often, glad that she had worked it out before leaving the house. Eager to begin rebuilding her network, she found a group of girls to go to lunch with, and took great care not to get too personal with them. Like her uncle had said, the town was booming, and therefore new kids weren't that unusual; she didn't even have to explain why she was there.

Catching her bus at the end of the day, she noted a boy she had met in a class took a seat on it as well. Watching him from the corner of her eye, she studied the wide holes in his ears that his gages held in place. She could also see the large silver ring he had placed in his nose, which had not been there earlier.

Noticing her stare, he smiled, "I have to take it out every morning and put it in after school. They don't let you wear anything but earrings on campus."

"That's stupid," she responded, moving to the empty seat next to him. "Have you been here long?"

"Naw," he shook his head slowly as he spoke, "My dad got a job here. Half the people I know are from somewhere else."

"I see," she gave him her smile, liking the way his dark hair stood on end, forming three inch tall spikes all over his head. *I've never had a boyfriend before, but I bet this guy would piss Uncle Pete off pretty good.* Keeping up the conversation, she pointed out on her map where she was headed, causing him to laugh.

"I live in those apartments, too," he indicated the general location of his family's dwelling. "They're new. We were one of the first families on the list; lived in a motel until then."

"A motel?" she widened her green orbs, feigning interest.

"Well; hotel. You know what I mean," he wrinkled his nose, pointing again, "Anyways, this is where we get on and off the bus." Arriving at their destination a few minutes later, they stood and exited the transport.

"See ya later," he called over his shoulder, his leaving her standing alone surprising.

Hmmm, he must be playing hard to get, she mused to

herself. Bailey had never dated by choice, but she never had a shortage of young men in pursuit of her. She called it keeping her options open, but in reality it had been done as most things were; to please her mother.

Glancing across the street, she could see businesses in the next block, which formed a huge strip mall. An enormous banner that read *Now Hiring* hung on the front of some type of eatery, judging by the tables and chairs on the patio in front of it. Her smile curling into a twisted sneer, she walked quickly to the corner to cross at the light and made her way to the door.

Inside, she asked for an application, which she quickly completed and returned to the counter. Taking it, the skinny kid at the register surprised her, "One sec, my boss wants to see you," so she gave him her smile, and stood to the side.

A moment later, an equally thin man in a dark blue shirt and bright red tie offered her his hand, "Hi, I'm Mark."

"Wow, I thought I would have to wait for a response," she informed him, breathing deeply while he steered her towards a booth.

"Oh, no," he chuckled slightly, "We need help, and finding it is hard to do around here."

"Is it? I wouldn't know, I guess. I just got here yesterday," she gave him a grin.

"I see here you have no employment history," he indicated the empty section with a pen.

"No, I've always done volunteer work back home. I

can provide some references, if that would help," she held the expression, growing nervous she might not get the job.

"That won't be necessary. Why don't you tell me about yourself?" he grinned at her encouragingly, and she didn't hesitate to fill him in on most of her essentials, only leaving out the reason she had made the trip to live with her uncle, or the fact that she wasn't with her parents.

Fifteen minutes later, he held out his hand and said crisply, "Congratulations, you're hired. When can you start?"

"When can you put me on the schedule?" she shot back evenly.

A slight rumble of laughter escaped his throat, "Nice. Tomorrow night, five o'clock. Here, let me give you a shirt, and you'll need a pair of black or khaki colored pants and white shoes. Oh, and don't forget the belt." Leading her to the back of the store, he handed her two red shirts. "And welcome aboard!" he shook her hand again heartily.

Stopping at the small boutique on the other side of the burger shop, she located two black pairs of pants and a belt to complete her uniform. Then, walking briskly to the apartment, Bailey used her key to get inside and rushed to the kitchen to pull a box out of the freezer.

So much for me being the maid, she quipped as she set the oven to preheat. *Guess he'll have to find his own damn way to cook dinner, since I'll be working.* Sliding the baking tray onto the rack and slamming the door, she grabbed her books and headed down the hall, swinging her auburn hair behind her.

SECRET LIVES

"You got a job?" Peter Mason demanded loudly between bites, "Why the hell would you get a job?" His voice resonated with angry accusation for a brief moment before he succeeded in reeling in his emotions. "I don't think that's a good idea, Bailey," he managed a calmer tone. "You've only been here a day, and you've got a lot of adjusting to do."

"Yes," she grinned sweetly, "And I've always had something to keep me busy," *and being house-mother isn't going to be it,* she tossed at him telepathically. "I won't overdo it, don't worry. But, you'll have to figure out what you're going to do about dinner, since I won't be here in the evenings." She smiled innocently, hiding her elation that she had succeeded at getting under his skin.

The man stared at her for a moment, then decided to let it go. "Well, in that case, the boys an' I will have dinner before we come home. That'll save us the time of cooking. Or, we'll work it out." *God damn it, I knew this bitch was gonna be trouble,* he glared at the girl, mentally stewing in his anger.

Turning to his nephews, "So, how was school today?" his tone immediately lightened when he addressed the youngsters. "Did you make some new friends?"

The twins eagerly joined the conversation, having stored up a full day worth of adventures. Peter smiled at the way the pair played off one another, filling in any gaps and painting a vivid picture of third grade life in Midland, Texas. Happy to have the distraction to keep him from making things worse with his niece, he and the boys retired to the living room for games and laughter as soon as the table had been cleared and the dishwasher set.

Leaving them to their controllers, Bailey made her way to her sparsely furnished room, and snatched her phone off the charger. She hadn't bothered to mess with Facebook or her friends much since her arrival, but after having a look around, she knew she needed the network.

I think I want a new profile though, she plotted as the system booted. *I don't want these kids here meshing with my friends back home; keep those boundaries clear.* Watching the little wheel spin, indicating the app was connecting, she waited. A minute later, she closed it and started it again.

"Well, damn," she cursed aloud when she noticed the small circle with a line across it at the top of the screen.

"No bars." Grabbing the knob and swinging the door wide, she stomped down the hall, "Hey, Uncle Darling, I have no service." She waved the device at him for emphasis.

Staring at her blankly, he considered her words for a moment. "Yeah, well, we'll have to get you switched over to my plan, I guess. Maybe this weekend we'll have time."

Her jaw dropped slightly, realizing it would be four days before she could do anything. "Why can't we go now?" she bit angrily.

"Because I'm busy now," he replied, turning back to the screen and unpausing the game, his attention back on the boys, "Ok, so what do I do with this thing?"

"You throw it," Jess continued to give his uncle directions, giggling loudly, "You suck at this, Uncle Pete."

"Hey, don't use that kinda language," his guardian reached over to poke him in the belly with a stiff finger, "An' I'm gettin' better."

Putting her hands on her hips, Bailey wanted to scream. *Sorry bastard,* she shook her head in disgust, realizing she had been dismissed. *He fawns over them like they were the best thing since sliced bread, and couldn't care less about me. I'm the extra baggage, so why doesn't he just send me home and be done with it?*

She slammed the door to her room as she sauntered inside. *That's what I'm gonna do. I'm going to make him*

SO REGRET making me come here. I was a nice girl, but those days are DONE. Flopping down on her bed and rolling onto her back, she turned the useless phone in her hands, thinking about the boy with the big ring in his face.

He's perfect. I need to get his name tomorrow and start working on how to get him over here so Uncle Dumbass can meet him. Chewing her lip, she continued to go through her day, analyzing the people she had met and her choices along the way. *I need a different group for lunch, too. Maybe nose-ring will have some friends and I can tag along with them.* They may have forced her to be there, but they couldn't tell her how to act or who to hang out with.

Reaching the part about her new job, an idea sprang into her mind, and caused her to giggle. *There's a phone store right down the strip from work. If I hurry tomorrow, I can get there early and find out about getting one for myself.* At the same instant, she realized that would be even better, as her uncle would be putting her old phone on his plan. *If he's keeping tabs on me, he won't know anything because my real phone will be private.*

She continued to smile at her deviousness, feeling proud of her plans for extracting her revenge. Tossing her useless cell on the nightstand, she stood and got ready for bed. Then, grabbing her books, she put her school work in order. Staring at one of the pages a few minutes later, she wondered how far she would be willing to go in her rebellion, but quickly decided failing classes wasn't something she was prepared to do; *at least not yet.*

At eight o'clock, Pete stood up to stretch and cut off the PlayStation, "That's it boys. Time for baths an' bed." He liked the way they grumbled slightly, and reassured them they would have plenty of time to play in the days to come. Herding them down the hall and into the bathroom, he felt almost happy to be settling into a routine with them. *If only their sister could be as compliant.*

Half an hour later, he tucked them in and switched off their light. Glancing at the room down the hall, he grimaced with an annoyed sigh. Reaching into his pocket, he pulled out a box of cigarettes. Smacking it against his palm a few times, he packed it, then opened the cellophane. Closing the front door behind him, he knew taking up the habit would make a good excuse for being outside whenever he needed to make a call.

Sliding one out, he flicked the lighter, then reached for his phone. Watching the smoke rise from the tip of his alibi, he listened intently, waiting for John Cross to pick up the line. "Hey bud, it's me."

"Yeah, I know," his old friend quipped, "Who else would it be? You left kinda sudden las' night," John observed.

"Yeah, I got interrupted. Listen, I need to make this quick. I'm gonna need someone after all," he drew a small drag and exhaled the cloud of smoke. "Let me know if you can swing it. She got a job, an' I'm gonna let her do her thing for a while; see if she'll settle in. I am gonna bring the boys this weekend, though. We can get started with them."

"Yeah, we can swing it. I already got my boy set up over there with you guys. I'll let him know. Where's she working?"

"Some burger place across from the apartment. You know, the one we ate at when we moved the furniture in here," Pete flicked some ash.

"Ai-ight. Anything else?"

"Nope. I won't call again, but you can leave me a message if you need to. Otherwise, I'll see you Friday night at the diner." He didn't wait for a response, ending the call and smothering the butt with his boot. On his feet, he noticed the blinds were swaying slightly in the narrow window next to the door, causing him to smile, *yeah, she's watching me.*

Back inside, Bailey in fact waited for him, having noticed he had gone out again. "I didn't know you smoked," she glared at him warily.

"Yeah, well, there's a lot o' things you don't know about me." He didn't look at her as he locked the door. "Go to bed, Bailey," he commanded, not wanting to fight with her. Lifting her chin, the girl made her exit, half-heartedly willing to comply.

Closing the door to his own room, Peter pulled his

shirt over his head, noticing the slight light-headed feeling he had picked up from his time on the porch. *Brenda'd sure be pissed if she knew I was smoking again.* He had kicked the habit years ago, after a great deal of prodding on his wife's part.

Standing at the dresser, he lifted an old wooden frame that held a picture of her. "I really do miss you, babe. An' I sure as hell could use you right about now." His wife had died from cancer three years before; his soul mate. It had been rough, but he had finally started to feel like his old self again. Or at least he had until he got a call from his mother that sent his world into a tail spin once again.

It had been nothing short of a miracle getting everything set up; something he would have to thank John for over the weekend. He had purchased a family vehicle, convinced his boss to allow him to move to an office job for a couple of months, and even had someone in the company help him secure the apartment. "Ungrateful wench," he muttered under his breath as he dropped his jeans and climbed into the shower.

The boys are happy though, his thoughts continued to churn. *And they'll make a nice addition to the group, after all. What we're gonna do with the girl, I don't know yet. I guess we'll have to wait and see if she can make it on her own.*

ON WITH THE SHOW

The following morning, Bailey rose early, getting dressed quickly and taking over the lavatory for her morning ritual. *Thank God Uncle Loser has his own,* meaning she only had to share with the boys. *One more thing I miss about home; my own bathroom.*

Observing herself in the mirror while she curled her crimson hair, she thought about nose-ring and what kind of girl he might be attracted to. *I may have to do an overhaul. Some black dye; maybe even pierce a few things myself.* She gave her reflection a crooked grin at the thought of being bad, and damaging her anatomy for the boy; *I'm sure it won't come to that.*

In the kitchen, her uncle had again prepared a nice breakfast for the two of them, but refrained from speaking to her, beyond a cursory, "Good morning."

Bailey only grunted a reply, eager to finish and get down to the bus stop to await her prince charming.

Gathering her things as soon as she finished rinsing her plate, she headed out the door and made her way across the compound.

The air felt a bit cool beneath the early grey light of dawn, and she stepped inside the small glass structure to take a seat on the bench. A few minutes later, she could see the young man making his way towards her, her breath catching in her nostrils at the smell of smoke that clung about him before she realized he still had the cigarette in his hand.

Grinning at her, he nodded before taking a lengthy drag, then using the glowing roll to indicate the approaching vehicle. "So, you like it here?" he bobbed his head slightly, dropping the butt in the receptacle by the door of the tiny hut.

"It has its perks," she gave him a slow smile, while tossing her crimson curls. Leaning slightly towards him, she cooed, "I never got your name. I'm Bailey," and offered him her hand at the same time.

He reached for her, clasping her fingers firmly, "I'm Ked."

"Ked?" she snickered. "That's an unusual name," she allowed him to hold her digits for a moment before pulling them away.

"Yeah, my parents named me Cedrick for some stupid reason. I don' like it, so my friends call me Ked," he grinned again, looking her up and down when she crossed in front of him to climb onto the bus.

Taking the window seat, Bailey wore a satisfied smirk when he sank down next to her, their arms brushing against one another. Making small talk, the pair arrived at the school a short time later and made their way to class. It turned out he was in the first two, and she easily wormed her way into his lunch crowd, catching a ride with them to a local sandwich shop.

On the ride home, she informed him about her new job, explaining that she had to hurry to change and get over to the store as soon as they were dropped at their stop. She liked the way he pouted slightly at the news, and made a point to lay her hand on his arm when she said her goodbyes, playing the flirtatious game new and thrilling to her. *I think I could get used to this,* she giggled to herself on the way up the stairs.

Changing clothes in record time, she jogged quickly to the corner to cross the busy street at the light. Arriving at the cellphone retailer, she felt relieved to be waited on right away by a young man with bright red freckles, but the joy was short lived. After she had answered a few questions, he let her in on the bad news, "You can't get a phone."

"What do you mean *can't*. I have the money, why can't I?" she practically stamped her foot in disgust.

"Well, you can, but you can't get one of these," he returned the model she had been inspecting to its holder. "Come this way," he curled his fingers, indicating for her to follow. "These are our pay as you go phones. There's no contract. This you can do; you just come in and pay your fee every month, and no one knows the difference."

Bailey crinkled her nose at the small selection, "Does it work like a regular phone?" She picked up a shiny silver one, turning it in her hand to see how it felt. "And why can't I get one of the regular ones?"

"Because you're not eighteen," the young man answered calmly, "Legally, you can't sign the contract. But… these work the same way, and have access to the same network. It's a little more expensive, paying month to month, but if you decide to skip a month for some reason, there's no penalty."

"Ok, I'll take it," she handed him the device, "But I can't do it right now. I'm going to be late if I don't get out of here."

"No problem," he nodded, pleased to make the sale, "I'll put it back for you, and get all of the paperwork ready. You want to come in after work?"

"I don't know what time I get off," she whined slightly, "But I can come again at the same time tomorrow to pick it up."

"Great! It'll all be ready for you when you get here. It won't take five minutes to close the deal."

Smiling, she clutched her oversized purse more tightly for a moment, rushing towards the door. Arriving at her place of employment at five on the dot, she huffed slightly, glad that he wasn't upset she barely made it. "I guess this'll take some getting used to," she panted.

"Get here as quick as you can," her boss agreed, "And don't make a habit of being late. You'll be fine. Now, let's get on those new employee forms, assuming you would like to get paid." Leading her to the back, he made copies of her ID and social security card.

Not sure what to put on most of the blanks, Bailey guessed at anything she wasn't sure of; especially the questions regarding dependents and taxes. *I don't plan on working here that long, anyways,* she rationalized, *although, having the income could prove useful.* Chewing the cap on the pen for a moment, she recalled that she had already begun making plans as to how she would spend her new wages, *so I guess I will see how it works out.*

When her paperwork was in order, the girl followed a fellow employee out to the front, where she was given the task of keeping the dining room in order. By ten o'clock, she felt exhausted and tired of the burger joint already.

Here I thought I was getting out of being the maid, she complained silently to herself as she wiped down her umpteenth table of the night. *Of course, I can't quit;* that would play into her uncle's wishes, which she would do anything to avoid. Noticing the last patron finally gathering his school books to leave, she looked at the clock; *thank God, we're closing.*

Mark called her over while he locked the doors, "So, how was your first night?"

"It was great!" she flashed a fake smile, "I can't wait to do it again tomorrow."

"Wonderful," he returned the grin, "Get your stuff out of the office and I'll let you out. And we'll see you at the same time, then."

Making a mad dash for the back, she opened her tiny locker and tugged on her bag until she had wiggled it out, giving the door a slam. "Good night," she bade her new employer at the exit, pausing to look up at the overcast sky when she was outside. Drawing a deep breath, she sighed, *well, I survived my first day,* while hearing the lock click behind her.

Crossing the street in the dark, she made sure to use the light, surprised at how much traffic still roamed about. *People in Texas must keep far different hours than they did back home.* Letting herself into the apartment, she discovered her uncle sitting in a recliner built into the end of the sectional sofa, bare chested and reading a magazine.

"Hey," she breathed, "You waited up for me?"

"Of course," he replied curtly. "I kept some dinner warm for you."

"Ah, thanks, but they let me eat at work," she made her excuse and scurried down the hall, closing her door gently behind her. The man had muttered *figures* under his breath as she left the room, putting a grin on her face. Dropping her purse on her desk, she quickly gathered her night clothes to take a quick shower and remove her makeup before she climbed into bed.

The following day amazingly similar, the young man at the cell store had her phone ready, exactly as he said he would. Placing it in her bag, she couldn't wait to get home and start to work on her new Facebook page. Being placed on dining room duty again, she sat to work clearing tables for the rest of the night, and her mind soon began to wander, with the ridiculously easy task she earned twelve dollars an hour to perform.

First, she thought about her new profile, and what she would put on it. Deciding that she wanted to be a different person than the Bailey she had always been, she devised several changes that would definitely be made. She also became a little sad she had already given her name as Bailey to her new classmates, since this would have been the perfect opportunity to change it if she had ever wanted to.

Eventually, her mind settled on her parents, and the fact that they had died so unexpectedly. They had never been a deeply religious family, even though she attended services from an early age. Bailey had begun to suspect years ago that doing so was all part of the act; all part of the front that the family presented to the world, and nothing more. Nonetheless, she wondered if they were in heaven, looking down upon her, and judging her actions.

A forlorn funk settled over her, and she wiped angrily at the grease spots and piles of ketchup left behind by the patrons. Allowed to eat a small meal during her fifteen minute break, she sat quietly, suddenly wishing she had been more choosy as to where she had taken employment. Cheese burgers and French fries might be every other teenager's ideal meal, but she was accustomed to finer restaurants where a waitress took your order at the table. *This will get old quick.*

Noticing a young man with spiky blond hair take a seat in the corner, she recognized him from the night before. *He's studying or something;* she eyed his books and papers as he got comfortable. *And he was the last one out last night.* Glancing at the clock and ending her break, she stood to dump her trash. Returning to work, she again became lost in thought, this time purposely avoiding her parents, and choosing to focus on the things that she could change about her life and future.

Closing time arrived eventually, and the young man gathered his things and left, seeming not to notice the girl who had bustled around him while he read. Again, her boss allowed her to grab her purse and take off as soon as all the tables were wiped down, but this time with the promise to teach her something new over the weekend.

"I come back at the same time tomorrow?" she inquired, realizing that it would be Friday. She suddenly wished she had the night off, in case Ked were to ask her on a date.

"Yes, only we close later, so you won't be getting off until midnight, both tomorrow and Saturday. After that, I'll have you on the regular schedule and you'll know your shifts ahead of time and can plan around it," he smiled at her when he spoke, obviously pleased at her performance thus far.

"Great," she managed her own grin. "I'll see you tomorrow then." Hearing the lock click in the door behind her, she made her way over to the light. Pressing the crosswalk button, she waited impatiently for the signal, then made her way to the apartment via the stairs. This time, her uncle wasn't waiting for her, but did come out of his room long enough to be sure she had closed and locked the front door behind her.

So what, she muttered to herself, alone in her room. *At least I finally get to work on my profile.* Making her shower quick and slipping into bed, she turned on the device and pulled up the app. She set up her new profile using the last name Mason instead of Dewitt; *like stone, I refuse to be broken.* She smiled to herself as she worked, and her bedside clock read well after midnight before she set it aside and finally fell asleep.

BIDING TIME

Bailey awoke later than usual the following morning. Frowning at the flashing red numbers, she cut off the alarm and rushed to the bathroom, getting dressed and hurriedly putting on her makeup. Not taking the time to curl her hair, she brushed out her auburn waves and twisted them up into a quick bun. Flying out to the kitchen, she sat down and devoured the morning meal, ready to leave and hopefully still make the bus.

"Not so fast," her uncle interceded. "I'll give you a ride this morning. We need to talk, anyways."

Bailey froze, petrified by what he might have discovered and want to discuss. Between the secret phone, Ked, and her plotting, she had become a nervous wreck. "Ok," she replied in a shaky tone, "Is everything ok?"

Peter picked up on the slight tremor in her voice, and wondered briefly if she had actually heard his conversation the other night when she had been watching at the window. "I'm taking the boys to The Ranch this afternoon; for the weekend in fact." He settled back into his chair, awaiting her response.

Bailey's jaw dropped, "The ranch? What ranch?" she demanded loudly, only taking a moment to piece a few things together. "You *really* don't live here, do you?" she accused.

"I do now," he responded calmly. "I had to rent the apartment so you guys would have a place to live and be able to attend school. I still have the place that Brenda an' I were building before she took ill. I'd invite you to come along, but I figure you'll wanna keep your job."

He didn't smile as he spoke, giving her a strange twist in her gut. "Yes, I want to go to work tonight. And they're expecting me to be there this weekend as well; they're going to train me."

"Well, then," he nodded, tapping the table with a stiff finger, "Here's the rules. Come straight home after work. Don't bring anyone inside the apartment, an' don't go anywhere else. That's it."

"What about my phone?" she snapped angrily. *If he's gone, I can't get my old phone back!*

Running his fingers around the outside of his mouth, Pete allowed the day's agenda to unfold before him. "Give it to me," he finally replied, "An' I'll go by and have it added to my plan. I'll leave it for you here on the table an' you'll have it when you get home tonight."

Rising, she moved slowly, her mind racing over what she had learned. Retrieving it, she recalled that before her parents' death, you never saw her without it; the link to all that she was before that fateful night. Returning to the small kitchen, she placed it in his hand, "Do you want the number?" she asked in a small voice.

"I have the number," he looked up at her, his face grim. "I really am sorry, Bailey. For everything." She could see his Adam's apple move up and down when he swallowed, his neck stretched from looking up at her. "Go on, see if you can make the bus."

At the bottom of the stairs, she broke into a run, her backpack and purse heavy and threatening to weigh her down. She felt a flicker of joy at seeing the transport pulling up at the glass shack.

Spying her coming down the front sidewalk, Ked chuckled and gave her a small wave. "Hey, can you hold up a sec?" he asked, indicating for the driver to wait for her.

Her face flushed when she climbed the steps, she flopped into the seat next to the boy and huffed, "Hi! Thanks for holding the bus."

"Don't mention it," he draped his arm around her for a quick hug, then allowed it to rest on her shoulders, testing the waters.

She smiled in response, aware that she liked the butterflies his touch produced. "What're your parents like?" she asked, out of the blue.

"My parents?" he stammered, surprised by her seemingly random question. "They're just parents, I guess. My dad don't spend much time at home; he works out in the oil field, seventy, eighty hours a week. My mom don't work. She's home all the time. I'm the only kid, so you could say they're a little disappointed," he lifted his free hand to indicate his appearance, "But whadda I care, right?"

Bailey grinned, "Exactly. My... stepdad... is taking my little brothers out for the weekend to visit some ranch, so I'll be home pretty much alone, starting tonight," her smile grew lopsided. "I have to work, but I was thinking maybe we could do something tomorrow, during the day."

Ked grinned, leaning in while pulling her closer, so that his face lay right next to hers. She could feel her heart pounding as if it would leap out of her chest when his lips made contact in a soft caress. "Sure, Bailey," he whispered, "I'd love to see more of you."

She laughed anxiously, and he sat back in his seat, removing his arm and wiping his palms on his pant legs. He couldn't believe he had lucked into meeting her, and felt amazed at how easy it would be to get into her bed; he was fairly certain that's why she had mentioned being unsupervised.

Stepping off the bus, the pair made their way into the building, pushing towards their first period. Scarcely having time to speak in their shared classes, they met at his friend's truck for the usual lunch run. Overcome by the sheer elation of his presence, Bailey dropped her bags when she got there, and threw her arms around his neck, using her tongue to kiss him.

Ked wasn't shy about the public display, and made a point to slide his hands down to feel her round rear end before she let him go. Lost in the giddiness he gave her, she felt light-headed when he released her; *he's so wrong, but he feels so right!* Sliding into the seat between the boys, the girl laughed merrily, eager to see what would happen next.

The following morning, which was Saturday, Bailey awoke to the silence of the empty apartment. Opening her eyes to stare at the bumps on the ceiling above her, she thought about her actions of the day before. She had behaved far out of character for her old self, allowing the boy to put his hands on her, and even going so far as to kiss him openly.

"You're playing a dangerous game," she warned herself into the grey light of dawn. She liked how it felt, though, finding the new Bailey far more exciting to portray than the old one. Climbing out of the bed, she had a shower and made her way to the kitchen for breakfast. She didn't go in to work until five, and the couple had arranged to meet at the bus stop at eleven-thirty.

He's going to show me around, she mused. *Take me to lunch, and all that.* Her plan seemed to be working perfectly, and she felt highly disappointed that her uncle had chosen to leave town for the weekend, as this would have been the perfect opportunity to introduce them. *I have to bide my time, I guess, until everything falls into place.*

Taking extra care with her hair and makeup, Bailey finally deemed herself ready and picked up her old phone to kill time while she waited. Pulling up her Dewitt Facebook account, she began to surf through old posts from her friends back home. Willing herself not to cry, she typed a few comments, hinting she might be returning some time, but leaving the idea vague for the moment.

Noting the time had come to leave, she gathered her things and laid her Dewitt phone on her nightstand with a sigh, her fingers lightly tracing the edge of her only remnant of home. Taking her wallet from her purse, she put a twenty in her pocket, along with her Mason phone, and locked the front door behind her.

At the bus stop, she sat on the bench, admiring the trees and shrubs along the front of the complex through the Plexiglas structure. Standing to meet her date when he arrived, she gave him a quick kiss and teased, "So, why is it you don't have a car to drive me around in?"

Toying with her fingers, he grinned in response, "Remember when I said my parents were disappointed in me? They won't buy me one until I get my shit together, as they put it. So, I take the bus," he laughed loudly. "How about you? Why don't you have a car?"

"Pete says we'll talk about it next year," she supplied shortly.

"Pete... your stepdad?"

"Yes," she nodded in agreement, sticking to the lie. "So where're we going?"

"The mall," he lifted her hand, kissing her palm.

"But since you're home alone this weekend, I was hoping we could check out your apartment, instead."

Bailey chewed her lip for a moment, stammering, "I'm almost alone. Not exactly alone."

"Uh-huh," he massaged her firmly before dropping the appendage, "Ok, then we go to the mall. There's lots to do there," he lied flatly; he had seen bigger and better malls when he lived in Houston. However, since it's all there was, he would take what he could get and hope for more down the line.

Seated on the bus, the couple held hands and made small talk, Ked mostly rambling about himself and sharing stories from his life. She noticed that he tended to exaggerate things, and had begun to find a few of his mannerisms annoying. *God, I hope I can keep it together long enough for Uncle Peter to at least meet him; this only works if he thinks we're a couple.* Eventually, she kissed him to shut him up.

Ked seemed quite willing to share in the physical interaction, his hands becoming bolder every time their mouths made contact. "I can't wait to get you some place alone," he breathed against her lips, "You're so hot, Bailey."

Pulling away enough to look him in the eye, she smiled, "We'll get there," she lied to his face, with no intention of sleeping with him, or anyone else for that matter. She had pledged to herself long ago that she would be a virgin on her wedding night. *But, he doesn't need to know that; it's all part of the plan.*

The bus dropped them off at the front of the food court, and the couple made their way inside. Deciding on Chinese, they ate, and then strolled through the extensive structure for the rest of the afternoon. Holding hands and laughing often, things appeared to be moving quickly for the young lovers. By the time they arrived at home for her to get ready for work, Bailey felt fairly certain she had the boy wrapped around her little finger.

LIKE YESTERDAY

Peter Mason unlocked the door, ushering his nephews inside their apartment. "Remember guys, don' tell Bailey about The Ranch. It's our secret," he reminded with a smile. He knew full well they were too young to obey such an order, and she would soon hear all about it.

"We won't," Jess offered, bouncing into the living area and turning on the television. "You gonna play with us, Uncle Pete?"

"I'm afraid I can't," his guardian replied, "I gotta get ready to start the new week. Head back to work tomorrow, an' all that." Leaving the boys to the entertainment system, he made his way down the hall. After five, he assumed that his niece would be at work, but to be safe, he knocked on her door and paused to listen.

Hearing no response, he twisted the knob and let himself in. Seeing her phone lying on the nightstand, he grimaced before picking it up and opening her Facebook. He had come across it when he had the phone activated, and had tried inspecting her page from his own while they were at The Ranch. In the end, her privacy settings were too high, and he couldn't see anything unless she friended him; an unlikely scenario.

Glancing around the room, he noticed that nothing seemed out of the ordinary, as he had already discovered his niece was as much of a neat freak as his sister had been. Her bed made and her clothes put away, he noted that she had even acquired an ironing board, which stood along the far wall. *I bet that was fun to carry on the bus,* he chuckled to himself. *Still, a good lesson for her.*

Closing the door behind him, he made his way down the hall to his own quarters, where he could inspect the device in private. Returning to her Dewitt page, he scrolled through, noting her latest post mentioned the possibility of returning to her old school. *Interesting.* When he first brought her to Texas, he wasn't sure how things were going to pan out. But, while he and her brothers had been on the long drive to the ranch, he had done a bit of soul searching.

In the end, he had decided that she needed to be there, where he could look after her. And therefore, the prospect of allowing her to return to her hometown was by all means, out of the question. *I have to figure out how to keep her here, for her own good,* he declared to himself. Shutting down the device, he returned it to its place beside her bed, then stood staring at it for a moment. *I wonder why she doesn't have it with her.*

The question bothered him the rest of the evening, while he cleaned the kitchen and the bathrooms, and did the laundry. Putting the boys to bed at eight, as usual, he wanted to call John's boy, to see how things were going, but he knew that was a bad idea. *He'll call me if anything important happens.* Otherwise, he needed to maintain his distance and keep his eye on the prize.

Taking his seat in the recliner a few minutes before ten, he waited patiently for his niece to arrive. When he finally heard her key in the lock, he pretended to be engrossed in his magazine, haphazardly lifting his gaze when she entered. "Well," he called to her quietly, "How was your weekend?"

"Uneventful," she replied calmly, dropping her purse on the ottoman, "How're the boys?"

"They're fine. Asleep already. They miss you, being away at work every night," he embellished.

"They don't miss me," she laughed quietly, "We hardly ever saw each other at home, why would they care now?" She stared at her uncle, wondering what he was up to. "How's the ranch?"

"Fine. Everything was the same as when I left it. I think we'll spend the summer there, so you'll have t' let your employer know you're gonna be away for a few months." He could see her eyes shift, and he tilted his head, "Don't tell me you'd rather work at a greasy dive than spend the summer with your family."

"I don't know what I'd rather do," she rolled her eyes at him. "It's still two months until school's out, so I don't see the point in even worrying about it right now," she scowled at her uncle, wishing she still had the house to herself. *Of course, if everything works with Ked, I won't have to worry about this summer.* "Anyways, I need to get my shower and get in bed."

Grabbing her bag, Bailey headed down the hall, not wanting to waste any more of her evening talking about things that only made her unhappy. Taking her night clothes, she slipped into the bathroom to wash her hair and body beneath the warm spray. Towel drying her auburn locks, she slid under her covers with a few damp tendrils clinging to her neck.

"Let's see what's going on tonight," she opened her Dewitt page, and scrolled through the news feed. *Nothing*, she breathed a deep sigh. Cutting her eyes over at the closed door, she stood and rummaged in her purse for her Mason phone, and opened the new page.

The newsfeed there was no more interesting, but held a private message, which made her heart rate increase with excitement as she read Ked's note... *Hey. Sorry I couldn't hang out with you today. I really missed you.* She smiled at the idea that he thought about her when they were apart.

Touching the screen to type a response, she messaged back... *I missed you, too. I'll be at the bus stop early tomorrow, so we can have more time alone.* Grinning to herself, she darkened the device and returned it to her bag, along with the Dewitt phone. Switching off the light, she curled up beneath the covers and drifted off to sleep.

The following morning, Bailey stuck to her plan, rising early and rushing to get her hair curled and makeup on. Making her way to the kitchen, breakfast wasn't quite ready, so she took her seat at the table, pulling out the Dewitt phone, and checking her Facebook page. Needing to maintain a few of her old contacts, she sent out some private messages while she waited, inquiring how things were going in her absence.

Peter noted her activity while preparing the meal, his tone surprisingly gently, "Keeping up with old friends? Or making new ones?"

"Both I guess," she answered noncommittally as he placed her plate before her. "The people here are alright I guess. I have a friend who rides the bus with me. It's nice."

Her uncle stifled the urge to pry, taking his seat and picking at his food. "At least you're moving on. That's what counts," he said with a smile.

Not bothering to reply, Bailey finished the eggs and toast, leaving her sausage on the plate. Standing, she gathered her things and headed out the door. Arriving at the bus stop, she found Ked already there and waiting for her in the fading darkness. "Hey," she called to him, dropping her bags on the bench.

"Hey yourself," he responded, grabbing her around the waist and pushing her back against the side of the small structure. His lips moving over hers, his hand found its way into her hair, massaging her scalp while he pressed himself against her. A moment later, he lifted his mouth long enough to breathe her name, and lean his forehead against her.

"I know," she whispered softly. "Trust me, I get it," she looked him in the eye and smiled. "It's going to be a long week."

"You think your old man'll go out of town again this next weekend?"

"I have no idea," she sighed, hugging him tighter against her, her heart pounding against her ribs, "But if he does, I want to spend it with you." She could feel her pulse in her neck, the thrill of him driving her insane. Never in her life before Texas would she have dreamed of kissing such a boy, and yet here she was, allowing him to fondle her in a very public place, should anyone be watching.

But who's going to be watching? she justified her actions. *It's still practically dark, and there aren't many people out and about at this hour to see.* Still, she had grown uncomfortable, and needed to slow down before they skipped school all together. Pushing on his chest firmly, she managed to put some space between them. "You're driving me crazy, you know that?"

He leered down at her, his fingers tracing her jaw,

"What, am I your first bad boy?"

Blinking at him for a moment, she rested the back of her head against the glass, "Yes, you are. And I can't say I don't like it, because I do. But it scares me."

Closing the distance, he kissed her hurriedly, aware of the bus slowly lumbering towards them, "I'm gonna get you, Bailey. I'm gonna get you hot, and naked, I swear to God!"

She trembled at the boldness of his words, finding them beyond comprehension, and her inability to calm her excitement even more so. She wanted to be sweet and innocent, like she had been before her parents died. But things were different, and she slowly understood that, like yesterday, those times were gone for good. *Please God, don't let Pete take the boys to the ranch again,* she pleaded silently, terrified, yet powerless to stop what might happen if he did.

THE TRUTH WITHIN

Bailey fumbled through the rest of the week. She had become caught up in the excitement of her romance with Ked, and thought of little else. The boy put his hands on her whenever they were close, and she made no effort to turn him away, almost craving it when they were apart. She knew it wasn't right, allowing herself to be pushed and pulled by the tide of desire.

By Friday, she had become a nervous wreck, dying to know if her uncle would leave her alone again, torn by what might happen if he did. That morning, at breakfast, she finally found the courage to inquire if they were going back to the ranch. Glaring at her plate, she couldn't bring herself to look at him when she asked, having realized they would probably use her bed when they did the deed, since his mother would be at his place.

Staring at the top of her head, Pete could tell something bothered her. "You know you can talk to me," he replied softly, taking his seat at the table. "If you need us to stay here, say the word. There's gonna be lots of weekends to go. Hey, why don't you tell your boss that you have to leave town, an' you can come with us," his tone shifted to hopeful.

She looked up to stare at him, curious how he could be so tender at that moment, as if she could feel his reaching out to her. "I'm fine," she lied calmly. "You guys go on, and have your fun." Her younger siblings had told her all about the horses, and the three wheelers. They had even mentioned a small, single engine plane that he had taken them for a ride in.

It sounded like a boy's paradise, but it held little attraction for her. "My brothers adore you. And your life. Take them to your ranch, and don't worry about me," she said quietly, returning her gaze to her unfinished meal.

Leaning on his elbows, Pete felt torn, knowing the boys had been talking to her since they got back. *I guess it hadn't been enough.* "It doesn't sound like I should leave you alone." He blinked at her, waiting for her response.

When the pause grew long, he tried again, "You know you'll never have your old life again. It's gone, and there's nothin' either of us can do about it," he shook his head slowly. "All you can do is make a new one, and that's how it is. The truth within you, who you really are, will never change, and can never be lost, so long as you hold on to it."

Reaching over, her uncle grasped her hand, giving it

a squeeze. "Do things you're proud of, Bailey. Don't let the sadness you're feeling drag you down, or make you do things you'll regret."

Her face shot up at his words, her green eyes staring into his soft grey orbs. "I won't," she promised quietly, afraid that he had seen her with Ked, waiting for the bus one of the mornings that week. *But that's what you wanted, isn't it? To get caught with him, so they would send you home, where you were safe?*

Suddenly, her plan seemed quite foolish, as if she had been playing with fire and was about to get burned. She sat studying her guardian, while her mind raced, trying to figure out what she should do next.

Pulling her hand free, she found her feet, "I had better go. I don't want to miss the bus." Grabbing her bags, she needed to get out of there before he said anything else she didn't care to hear.

Fumbling through a long and boring day at school, Bailey's mind often returned to the conversation she had shared with her uncle. Not paying attention during most of her classes, she allowed herself to run through scenarios of what could, or probably would, happen between the boy and herself.

Each time she reached the scene where the two of them would be completely alone, she became a little more confident she would not allow it to happen. *But how do I stop it?* she asked herself over and over, realizing if she did, all her work to get him would have been for nothing.

Riding the bus home, she pretended like everything was fine, and kissed the young man quickly before she made her dash to prepare for work. She had excelled in her register training, and Mark put her on the front again that night, much to her relief. He had praised her ability to count, which made her laugh, as she had assumed that everyone could, but apparently not.

To her surprise, Ked showed up at her counter shortly before closing and ordered a coke, then made himself at home in the lobby to wait for her. As time ticked down, she slipped her way out and took a seat across from him, whispering loudly, "What the hell are you doing here? Are you trying to get me fired?"

"Get you fired?" he held up both hands innocently, "No, baby, I just needed to see you. Your old man's gone, right? I told my mom I was staying over at a friend's house…" he let the sentence drop, giving her a smile, and she quickly deduced that she was the friend.

Panic washed over her, and her eyes darted around the deserted dining area, catching sight of their usual late night patron. "Get out!" she managed through gritted teeth, "Go outside, and we'll talk about this when I get off. I should be out in about fifteen minutes, thirty at the most." Standing, she stomped to the back, hoping he would obey her.

Turning around, she could see that he had in fact followed directions, and the blond busily packed his things as well. Licking her lips nervously, she went through the steps of preparing her register, and restocking the front. Finally having everything in order, she grabbed her purse out of the back, and asked Mark to let her out.

She found Ked waiting for her at the stop light, hands in his pockets and staring at the moon. "I'm sorry that I screamed at you," she said quietly as she approached.

"Yeah," he smiled down at her, "I'm sorry that I surprised you. I didn't mean to get you in trouble." Pulling his left arm free, he hung it across her shoulders, and she leaned against him as they crossed the street and walked down the sidewalk towards the complex. "I should have asked you before I made plans for tonight."

Bailey grew tense, aware that she was alone; *very* alone. "You can't stay with me Ked. I told you I wasn't really alone," she tried to sound convincing.

"So, is your mom still here? You know, you ain't said much about your family... I'm beginning to wonder if you really have one." He stopped moving, the shadow around them making him practically invisible in his dark clothing.

"Yes, I have one," the irritation returned to her voice, "And I have to get home shortly, before I'm missed." Looking up, she stared into his angry eyes, "Just go home, Ked. Tell your mom that your friend is an asshole and you got into a fight. Tell her you decided to sleep in your own bed."

"Ok," he agreed reluctantly, his lips curling

downward, "But you said a few minutes. Let's say goodnight first," he twisted them into a smile, sliding his hands up her arms and around her back. His mouth pressed to hers, her resolve softened, allowing him to deepen the kiss. Slowly, he inched between the shrubs along the edges of the walkway and worked her towards the building.

When her spine met the brick wall, she felt a brief surge of excitement, hiding in the shadows with him and his body pushing against hers. A moment later, panic gripped her; his fingers had found flesh and tickled her waist. "Ked, stop," she managed to free herself enough to protest, before he reclaimed her, holding her in place while he continued to pull at her clothing, trying to force her onto the ground behind the short bushes.

Falling, Bailey hit the earth beneath her, bruising her knees as she went down. Rolling onto her back, she flailed her limbs wildly, the weight of him making it hard to breath. She emitted a loud shriek, and a hand clamped over her mouth, pressing her cheek painfully against her jaw and teeth.

Desperately sucking air through her nose, she fought to remove the digits blocking the passages. She could hear the material of her shirt as it tore away from her body, leaving her bare skin exposed. Suddenly, cold air rushed over her while another man's voice cursed loudly, followed by the sound of blows landing in the darkness.

Fighting to sit up, she peered over the green leaves of

the hedge and worked to cover herself with what remained of her top. Staring in stunned silence, she watched two forms wrestle about in the pale moonlight, one of them taking one hell of a beating, fearing that it was Ked. Frozen in place, her mind screamed that she should run, but her limbs shook, and she simply cringed, too frightened to stand, let alone flee.

Moments later, one of the shadows stood, while the other lay motionless on the path. "You ever touch 'er again, I'll kill you!" her defender lay down his threat evenly, kicking the limp figure for good measure. Turning to the girl, he climbed over the brush, grabbing her roughly and dragging her to her feet, "Can you stand?"

Hot tears of recognition streamed down her flushed cheeks, "Oh, my God!" she clung to him on weak knees, "I think so," she told the blond patron from the restaurant. "Please, take me home."

"Not sure which way's home," he replied crisply, "But I can sure 's hell get you outta here." Lifting her into his arms, he carried her around the turn and along the walkway, stopping to rest her on a flight of steps.

Looking about, she gasped, "Thanks… but we're on the wrong side of the complex." Giving him her apartment number, she continued with a firm declaration, "I'm ok, I can walk. But my purse is back there… in the flowerbed."

"Don't move," he commanded. Retracing their steps,

he grabbed the oversized bag and returned to her, huffing, "That guy's gone." Helping her to her feet, he chided, "You might consider carryin' something a little smaller. Maybe somethin' you can swing." He laughed quietly at his own joke, bringing a faint smile to her lips while she rested against him.

Leaning on her rescuer, she hobbled along until they arrived at the correct building, and she climbed the stairs gingerly. At the top, she rummaged in her purse to locate her keys, while stating more calmly, "Thanks for saving me." Brushing away the tears and dirt from under her eyes, she glanced at the man behind her anxiously.

"Don' mention it," he replied with a toothy grin, "But I strongly recommend an escort from now on."

"Yes," she agreed with a small smile of her own. "You could be right about that."

"You want me t' stay, an' wait for the police with you?" he asked quietly, brushing her long locks out of her face.

"No," she shook her head and took a step back, "No police." She glared up at him, thoughts of trying to explain her relationship with Ked flashing through her mind. "I'm ok, and you took care of him. I think it's over with."

"You knew that guy, didn' you," his jaw grew tight, fresh anger taking its toll.

"Yes, I know him, but it's ok. I'm sure it wasn't entirely his fault," she lifted her chin, "And it won't happen again."

Picking up on her fearful vibe, the stranger nodded, "Well, I'll be off then, as soon as you're inside." He held a hand up, fingers stiff to indicate the passage behind her.

"Ok, yes, thanks!" she fumbled to insert the key in the lock. "I guess I'll see you at the shop," she swung the door open and stepped inside, "Tomorrow night?"

"Sure," he nodded, giving her a small salute, "Now, close the door, an' don't you dare open it for anyone."

"Don't worry, I won't," she replied, closing the portal with a light slam and sliding the deadbolt into place before sinking to the floor and sobbing into the darkness.

A FINE MESS

Bailey leaned closer to the mirror and inspected the bruises; *damn*. She could almost see the fingerprints in her flesh where Ked's hand had pressed against her jaw, covering her mouth. *How could I be so stupid?*

Of course, she had been right the night before, when she said it wasn't entirely his fault. She had been leading him on, pretending she intended to sleep with him. Deep down, she feared that she actually might have, or at least wanted to, despite knowing it would be wrong. *I liked the way I felt when he held me*; as if all her problems dissolved in his arms. Closing her eyes, she became lost for a moment, shuddering at the conflict the memory produced.

No wonder the preacher always warned us against having sex outside of marriage. Grabbing her bottle of liquid foundation, she squeezed it angrily. *You've made a fine mess out of things, Bailey Ann Dewitt.* At least her physical innocence had been preserved, if not her mental stability.

Covering the marks, she dusted her face with powder, frowning at the shadow still visible beneath the cover. *Maybe no one'll notice.* Continuing with the rest, she was soon presentable. Putting on her second shirt, she realized she would either have to wash the one every night, or ask for a replacement.

Holding up the remains of the garment, she frowned at the memory of having it forcibly removed the night before, while she formulated an excuse. *I spilled bleach on it. That should convince Mark to give me another one.*

Heaving a deep sigh, she dropped the remnant in the kitchen trash, then stared at it, realizing she would have to carry it out so that her uncle didn't see it. Her face flushed at the thought of him knowing what she had done. Based on their last conversation, she suspected he already knew.

Grabbing the bag, she unbolted the door and made her way to the dumpsters on the back side of the property. Her eyes roaming, she kept a lookout for Ked, or anyone else, and wished she knew which apartment belonged to him so that she could avoid the area.

A few minutes later, she locked her door, safely back inside. Preparing a meal for herself, her thoughts continued to churn, until she finally forced them away; *enough wallowing. What's done is done, and we can only move on from here.*

Washing her dishes after she ate, Bailey couldn't stand being in the apartment alone any longer. Grabbing her purse, her mind flashed to her rescuer, recalling his advice about getting a smaller one, and she grinned at the thought of him. *Lucky for me he was on his way home, and saw the commotion.*

Making her way down the stairs, she clutched the bag anxiously, and followed the path to the front of the complex. With the street to her right, she refused to look over her shoulder at the small glass structure where the couple waited for the bus each day, and instead remained focused on the streetlight ahead of her.

Crossing at the intersection, she entered the store and exhaled loudly in relief, instantly aware that she had been holding her breath the entire journey. Spying her knight in shining armor, she shifted her weight while trying to decide her next move. He had obviously not noticed her arrival, and still stared at the book and pages before him.

Making her choice, Bailey moved slowly towards his table, stopping next to him. Timidly reaching over, she tapped the laminate coating, and he looked up at her, a startled expression on his features before he broke into a small smile.

"Why, hello," he breathed airily, mentally noting the dark smudges around her pretty mouth, "Glad t' see you made it in t' work today."

"Yes, I made it. I'm early in fact," her lips curled slightly in return. "Would you mind if I sat down?" she indicated the leather covered bench across from him.

"Not at all," he shoved the papers into the book and closed it. "I'm Caleb, by the way; Caleb Cross."

"Bailey," she replied shyly, offering him her hand as she sank down into the seat, "Bailey Dewitt."

"Bailey," he repeated, "I like that name. So, are you a student? Or are you here with your family?" He smiled warmly, inviting her to open up, but he could see her reluctance. "It's ok if you don' wanna talk; after last night, I get it if you don't."

"No, I'm fine," she avoided looking at him by staring at the material he had been studying. "I'm just in a hard place right now; in my life. What I could really use…" she drew a deep breath, pausing for a long moment. "What I could really use right now is a friend. A real one."

Caleb nodded, looking out the glass to his right, "Ok, then I guess we're off to a good start." Shifting his gaze to meet hers, he teased her with a half-smile, "I'm Caleb, and I'm here because of work." He indicated the outside with an open palm, "This area's boomin', an' I came here for th' money. I also thought it would be a great idea t' take some college classes online in my spare time," he leaned back in his seat, running the hand through his short blond hair, exhaling through tightly drawn lips.

"You're not enjoying it?" she asked, intrigued by his obvious frustration.

"Well, not really. Anyone who tells you that takin' a

class online is easy is lyin' t' you. They take twice the work, an' ten times the dedication."

"I noticed," she grinned with a small nod, "I mean, you're here every night, working on that book," she indicated his nemesis with a flick of her hand.

"Yeah, it's kicking my ass, too," he showed her his full set of perfect white teeth, "I go t' work every day for ten or twelve hours, then I come in here t' study for a few more before I head home, get some sleep, an' do it all over again."

Bailey could feel an odd tingle in her palms, her face growing tense at some dark realization in the back of her mind, "Why don't you study at home?" She unconsciously darted her eyes towards the stoplight, thinking about the apartment he surely held in her complex.

Caleb inhaled sharply, following her thoughts haphazardly, "Home isn't very comfortable," twisting his tongue he confessed, "I don't live in those apartments." He could see the shock on her face, and knew he was on dangerous ground, so he opened his palms towards the ceiling, as if to surrender to her, "I was only there last night... because I followed you."

Bailey's face scrunched in angry disbelief, "What the hell do you mean, you followed me?"

"I didn't like the looks o' that guy," he replied, staring at her calmly. "The two o' you had words, remember? And, I couldn' let it go. So I went out after him, an' I waited." He finally broke his eye contact, shifting back to the scenery outside with a shrug. "I figured I would follow an' make sure you made it home ok."

The silence between them grew thick, each of them mentally retracing the events that followed his choice. On the one hand, the girl was glad that he had been there; but on the other, the circumstances of it brought panic to her raw and wounded existence. "I have to clock in," she said, standing.

"I'm sorry," he muttered as she made it to her feet, "I didn' mean to upset you. I'd rather not lie to you, though." He looked at her again, her green eyes sharp, piercing him with their distrust. "Have a good night, Bailey."

"Yes, you have one as well," she remembered her manners, throwing her bag over her shoulder and making her way to the back. Moving in a dazed state, she paused in the office long enough to adjust her clothing and check her makeup and hair. *Girl, you need to stay the hell away from guys,* she admonished her reflection in the mirror, *'cause you definitely have a way of attracting the weirdoes.*

NO PLACE LIKE HOME

Peter Mason had always thought there was no place like home; home being The Ranch. He and his wife, Brenda, had bought the land before they were married, and had spent seventeen years building, turning it slowly into their palace before she had been diagnosed with cancer. The Lord had taken her only a year after that, and during that time, they had spent very little energy working on the property, and most of it fighting for her survival. In the end, they lost.

Gripping the wheel on the drive back to Midland, he glanced at the boys in the mirror. They intently viewed the screen above them as it displayed one of their favorite movies. The first weekend he had taken them out, he had been relaxed and eager to be there; happy to introduce them to the life that wasn't theirs yet, but soon would be.

This weekend, he couldn't seem to find the same focus, and part of his attention constantly returned to the apartment and the girl he had left there. *I wish to God she hadn't been part of this deal.* But his heart kept telling him she needed a place to belong; *deserves it as much as these guys do.*

Shifting his eyes back to the road, he inhaled deeply and allowed the breath to slowly escape; *I'm sure she's fine.* However, he had an uneasy feeling that she wasn't, and had packed the boys up early, in a rush this time to get home and check on her.

Mentally retracing what had happened since the fateful call that had bound all of their lives on a new course, he knew the girl hated him. *Or what I represent, in the least,* he corrected himself. *She doesn't want to be here, and I don't blame her.* Pete knew the pain that his older charge faced, and what it would take for her to overcome it.

Pulling into the parking area, he found an empty spot and climbed out to help the boys, "Alright gentlemen, get all your stuff an' take it inside." He grinned, watching them gather their trash, aware that his sister had in fact done a fine job of raising them, despite the differences the two of them had shared. *She was a good mom; I gotta give her that.*

At the top of the stairs, he stopped and surveyed the ground below him, not really comfortable surrounded by the buildings that made up the rest of the complex. Deep down, he knew it had been the right thing to do, getting the apartment so Bailey could finish school. However, after next year, he fully intended to take the boys and move to The Ranch permanently, where they would be home-schooled, along with the rest of the children in his small, close-knit community.

Making his way inside, Pete could feel his pulse in his neck, his instincts on edge. He knew that his niece had been behaving strangely, and quickly concluded her actions held deception. She had started leaving much too early to catch the bus, and he wondered where she actually went for the extra fifteen or twenty minutes each day. *Not that it's enough time to get in any real trouble,* he debated with himself. But still, he could not resist the feeling that something wasn't right.

Making his way to the back of the apartment, and his own room, he noted that the place was deserted, and the girl nowhere in sight. *Surely she didn't go in to work this early; it's barely after four.* Gathering the laundry, he tried to put his mind at ease by taking care of some chores. Tackling the bathrooms, his thoughts continued to darken his mood, and eventually he gave up.

"Come on boys," he called loudly, "It's dinner time. Maybe we can eat over at Bailey's work an' surprise her," telling himself at the same time he wasn't really checking up on her; *we're just going to eat.*

Standing in line a few minutes later, Peter did his best to hide his relief that she was indeed where she should be. "Hey, Bailey-girl, what's good in this place?" He spoke warmly, holding his smile in place as a look of terror crossed her features.

"Uncle Peter!" she replied breathlessly, "What're you guys doing here? I thought you would be at the ranch until tomorrow!"

"We decided to cut the trip short," he explained her confusion away, "So give us three dinners, preferably somethin' these guys will like." He teased her slightly, pulling out his wallet and handing her his card, "You look a little tense; is everything ok?"

Swiping the plastic and handing it back quickly, she stammered, "Everything's fine. Your number's four-eighty-six. They'll call you shortly." Turning her attention to the next person in line, she dismissed her relation without another word.

Taking their cups, Pete led the boys into the dining area where they prepared their drinks and chose a table. Sliding into his chair, he noticed the blond man who watched them intently, and gave him a short nod. The crowded dining room seemed a bit noisy for studying, but he noted that the young man seldom looked up from his thick book and stacks of paper.

Eight hours later, Bailey stepped out into the night air, shivering slightly.

"You cold?" a familiar voice pierced her thoughts, and she spun around to face Caleb squarely.

"What the hell are you doing here?" she demanded loudly. "Maybe I didn't make myself plain earlier, but you have no business following me!"

"Relax, Bailey," he shifted his backpack higher onto

his shoulder, "I'm not gonna hurt you. I jus' wanna make sure you make it home, ok?" He stared at her with steel grey eyes that cut through the dim light.

Chewing her lip slightly, she considered banging on the glass and asking for help, but something about his flat calm told her she was being foolish. "My uncle's at home, waiting for me," she said loudly.

"Ok," he bobbed his head, "Sounds good. I wadn't plannin' on goin' in; I'm walkin' ya t' the door."

Lifting her chin, Bailey pushed past him and headed towards the stop light to punch the button and wait for the signal to change. Clutching her purse, she tried to get more details on her self-appointed bodyguard, noting that he stood about six foot tall, and appeared heavily muscled in build; *no wonder he had taken Ked down so easily.*

Of course, I bet Caleb has a bit more experience on top of being bigger. "How old are you?" she demanded with a huff as they reached the other side of the street.

"I'm twenty-one," he kept his reply short, hoping to rebuild her trust. She cut her eyes over at him, taking long strides in her haste. "How old are you?" he asked, noting they were approaching the darker shadows where she had been attacked the night before.

Bailey swallowed hard, determined to walk down the path and not let her fear get the better of her. "I'm sixteen," she replied smoothly. "My birthday falls the last week of school most years, and I'll be seventeen."

"So, you're a junior?"

"Yes, I'll be a senior next year, and then I'm off to college," she couldn't keep the excitement from her voice, relieved to have reached the stairs to her balcony. "Well, here we are. Thanks for walking me home." Her words were clipped, and she didn't wait for a reply, mounting the steps and stomping up them loudly, leaving him in the darkness below.

Inside, Bailey shut the door, letting out a startled squeak, which she quickly stifled, "What're you still doing up?" It was half-past midnight, and she had fully expected him to be asleep.

Peter sat staring at her, reclined in his favorite location. He still wore his jeans, but had removed his shirt, exposing his tuft of greying brown chest hairs, another of his habits the girl found irksome. He closed his magazine slowly, taking his time, and not giving her a response.

Bailey shifted nervously, unaccustomed to seeing half-naked men, even ones related to her, "Can you at least put a shirt on? You know, we didn't parade around our house half-nude! You're setting a terrible example for the boys!"

"I'm sure you didn't," her uncle nodded slightly, "You're parents were a bit uptight about all sortsa things." Tossing the glossy pages aside, he indicated the other end of the couch, "Why don't you have a seat; let's have us a little talk."

"A talk? About what?" she spit at him, growing angry that he refused to comply with her request.

Leaning forward, Peter rested his forearms on his knees, "The bruises on your face, for starters. Have you been in a fight?"

Bailey's mouth fell open, and she made a loud gasping noise, wrinkling her nose in protest, "Bruises? What the hell are you talking about?"

Leaping to his feet, his voice boomed, "Siddown!"

Trembling, the girl slid around the end of the sofa and perched on the edge of the brown cushion. "Ok, I'll sit," she stammered, "You don't have to shout. You'll wake the boys!"

"The boys're fine," he said through clenched teeth, "It's you I'm worried about."

"Me? Really, I'm ok!" she lied without hesitation.

He ran his fingers through his sandy waves, "No, you're not. But you're too young to see it." Sitting, leaning on his arms again, Pete's voice softened, "Now, from the beginning. What happened to your face? And don't leave anything out."

Staring at the man before her, Bailey could feel the moisture building in her eyes. She couldn't remember the last time she had gotten in trouble; for any reason. She had always been a good girl, and having people raise their voices at her was something she had rarely experienced.

Finally, after a few minutes of internal struggle, she tried to explain, "I can't tell you." A tear spilled over and rolled down her cheek. "All I can say is I'm sorry. I know that I screwed up, and it won't happen again."

Shaking his head, Pete folded his hands, rubbing them together, "I wish I could believe that," his voice low, almost a whisper, "But this is a big responsibility, an' I can't afford to screw it up. Please; tell me what happened."

Drawing a ragged breath, the floodgates opened and she sobbed, wiping at the streams angrily, "I told you, I screwed up. I met a boy, and was stupid, and he thought... and I let him think... and when I changed my mind he got all upset." She could see her uncle's hands clenched into fists.

"Stop being pissed off!" she bit sharply, "It's over; it's done with! And I probably won't ever see him again!" she flung the words at him, in the same instant aware that she would see him again, Monday morning in fact, when they got on the bus. The realization froze her features in horror, and she knew that she was sunk.

"I'm taking you to school in the mornings," her uncle replied firmly. "And I'll be there to pick you up when it lets out. I'll walk you to work, and afterwards I'll be there to pick you up."

"You can't do that! What about the boys? They need to be in bed by the time I get off work!"

He stared at her for a moment, wanting desperately to

demand that she quit her job, but knowing it would be a mistake to make such a request. Swallowing, his Adam's apple moved up and down, and he folded his hands in front of his face to tap on his lips with the edges of his fingers, obviously lost in thought.

Seeing her opportunity to make amends, she began to plead, "I promise. I won't get in anymore trouble. You can pick me up from school, and take me. I'll go straight to work, and come straight back, and Caleb can walk me home again, too!"

"Who's Caleb?" he demanded wryly.

Oh, shit! Her mind jolted to an abrupt stop. "He's... another guy," she replied lamely, suddenly aware that her plan had been wrong from the start and that going home to her grandmother had never been an option, no matter how much trouble she got into. "Look, uh... can I go get a shower, please? I promise I'll tell you everything, as soon as I get out."

"You've got ten minutes," he replied curtly while rising to his feet. Grabbing the pack of cigarettes off the table, he slammed the front door behind him.

POKER FACE

Bailey removed the makeup from her flesh, and examined the lines that were easily distinguished on her left cheek; they looked like fat fingers. Exhaling a deep sigh, she turned on the water, and took her shower, washing her auburn locks, and allowing the warm cascade to flow over her. Leaning her head against the wall, she wanted to cry, surprised to find the tears that had fallen like rain only moments before seemed to have been spent.

A loud bang at the door startled her, and she lifted her chin, "Yes?"

"Time's up!" her uncle's voice called from the other side.

"Ok," she replied weakly, turning the valve and grabbing her towel. A few minutes later, and dried for the most part, she put on her pajamas. Taking the cloth with her to dab her damp hair, she made her way out to the front room, where she could see him setting up the coffee pot through the window. Moving to stand at the table, she obediently waited for him to look at her. She no longer felt afraid of what he would say; whatever it was, she deserved it.

Turning to face her, he indicated the table before he noticed her bruised cheek, the handprint dark against her pale flesh, and demanded loudly, "Did Caleb do that to you?"

"No!" she shook her head profusely, "Caleb saved me. He pulled Ked off of me... and beat him up."

"Ok," Pete's hands shot up to his hips, "So who's Ked?"

Bailey hung her head as she pulled out a chair, "Ked's a boy from school. He's got these giant rings in his ears and wears one in his nose, too." She stared at her lap as she described the events, recalling what she could, and then sitting quietly, waiting to receive her uncle's wrath.

After the pause grew long, Peter got to his feet and poured himself a cup of the hot liquid. "Would you like some?" he asked calmly.

Looking at him, Bailey could see the frown on his profile, "I'll take a glass of water. I don't really like coffee."

"Good girl," he praised, turning to the fridge to fulfill her request. "So," he sat the drinks on the table and reclaimed his seat, "What should I do about this?"

She stared at him with wide eyes, "Why the hell are you asking me?"

"Because you're the one who fucked up," he stated forcefully. Drawing a deep breath, he struggled to keep his composure, "An' since I'm brand new t' the whole parent business, I thought I'd find out what you had in mind. What would they do about this?"

Bailey stared at him, her tear supply renewed, "I would never have done this to them." Her lip quivered, and she begged, "I'm so sorry, Pete. Please forgive me!"

"Aww, honey," he reached for her, clasping her fingers and cupping them between his hands, "We all make mistakes." He had feared she was acting out because her parents were dead, and having the suspicion confirmed didn't make him feel any better. "So when you got into trouble, how'd they punish you?"

She stared at him, swallowing hard, "I never got into trouble. I did… what they expected me to do. I had my friends, and my own life, and they pretty much left me to it."

"An' now all that's gone," he finished for her.

"Yes," she wriggled her digits away from him. "I feel… really lost right now. Part of me wants to go home, but deep down, I don't think that would fix any of this. They're gone; and they're not coming back."

Peter stared at the girl with a perfect poker face, his raw emotions completely unreadable. It had been three years since he lost his bride, and it had taken him the better part of that time to make it as far as this girl had done in a matter of weeks. "No," he finally managed to reply softly, "They aren't. It's down to us; you, me, an' the boys. We have to make the best of it, 'cause there aren't many options left, if we can't make this work."

"Then we have to make it work," she agreed with a sniff.

"Ok," he slapped the table with an open palm, "I'll be taking you t' school an' picking you up. I'll allow you to walk to work, an' walk home, but I expect to find you where you're supposed to be at all times, an' believe me I'll be checking! And I want you to stay away from this Ked character. Don't talk t' him, period!"

"What about Caleb?" she asked softly.

"I don't know. Tell me about him," he folded his hands impatiently, his irritation still evident.

"He comes to the shop every night to study. He's taking some class, and he has a job. I talked to him yesterday, when I got to work, and he seems nice. He said he wants to look out for me, and he walked me home last night."

"So, where does he work?"

"I don't know. I didn't ask," she avoided telling him that she had cut their conversation short when Caleb had given her the creeps by admitting to following her home.

"Then I wanna meet him," Peter replied stubbornly.

"Ok, he's at the shop every day, like I said. You can

come over there, and talk to him, or if he walks me home tomorrow night, I can ask him in to meet you." The idea of the second scenario gave the girl an odd feeling in the pit of her stomach, and she hoped that would not be the course of action her uncle preferred.

"I'll come t' the store," he finally decided, noting that the girl exhaled loudly at the news, as if she had been holding her breath. "What time does he arrive?"

"It's really hard to say," she shrugged, "It's different times. Maybe at eight or nine you could come over. I'd say that he'll be there by then."

"Alright, then it's settled. I guess you can head off t' bed."

Getting to her feet, Bailey could feel a lump that remained in her gut. Things may have been settled, but for her they were far from over. Slowly making her way to the sink, she emptied her glass, and placed it in the dishwasher.

"Bailey," her uncle called her softly, and she lifted her chin to look at him. "I know who Caleb is," he said with a short nod.

Her green eyes grew wide, and she could feel the flush crawling up from her chest, "What do you mean, you know who he is?"

"He's the son of a friend o' mine," Peter blinked rapidly, "I arranged for him to come to help me keep an eye on you, since I wasn't really sure how you were going to behave; especially after you took a job the second day you were here."

"You mean you had him… spying on me?" her disbelief evident, her eyes narrowed in anger.

"Yeah," he nodded, toying with his half empty mug. "I wanted to see if you would lie to me. Or if you were gonna be honest." He shrugged, not sure if it was a wise choice to reveal their connection. He knew she would discover it eventually, and saw no point in continuing the farce. "You have Caleb walk you home every night, an' he'll watch out for you."

"Anyone else I should be on the lookout for? Any other spies who'll be reporting on me?"

"No," he clipped the word crisply, "Just Caleb. My best friend's son."

"Well, I'm glad we got that out in the open, then. And I guess this is goodnight." Bailey didn't wait to hear any more, and stomped out of the room. Her family had always been centered on respect and honesty. Closing the door to her bedroom, she flopped down on her bed, and stretched out on her belly, turning her head so that she could see the nightstand beside her.

And here I thought I was the one being deceitful, she grumbled to herself, staring at the long edge of her Dewitt phone in disgust. *But it turns out, ol' Uncle Pete was on to you from the beginning.* Or rather, didn't trust her from the beginning. Closing her eyes, she drifted off to sleep, not sure if things had been resolved, or if her troubles had only just begun.

KEEPER

Bailey sat on her bed, listening to her brothers' laughter in the front room. They were playing one of the games that Peter had provided for them, and making quite a ruckus about it. Slipping into her jeans and a tee, she crept down the hall in her bare socks to peek in on them.

Standing at the entrance to the living area, she could see the giant screen of the television. Her eyes grew wide as she realized that one of them played a sniper, shooting people at a distance and laughing as blood squirted from their heads.

"What the hell are you doing?" she blurted out, stomping into the room, "This doesn't look like a game for kids!"

Startled by her sudden appearance, Jess leapt to his feet, "It's ok, sis, Pete got it for us!" He looked so small, standing before her and waving his hands to emphasize his point, "It's called Call of Duty and it's about saving people."

"Saving people," she spoke loudly, "It looks like it's about killing people!" Anger boiled over inside her, and she whirled around, prepared to confront her uncle about his choice of entertainment for her young siblings.

"What seems to be the problem?" Peter spoke calmly from the hallway behind her while using a towel on his freshly washed curls.

"The problem?" she shrieked, "You let them play this? This crap isn't fit for anyone, much less a pair of nine year old boys! Are you out of your ever loving mind? They're shooting people!"

"They're not real people," he replied snidely, moving past her and making his way into the kitchen. Dropping the towel on the back of a chair, he began pulling things out of the fridge and placing them on the counter. "You boys want pancakes today?"

"Yes!" they sang out in unison, not missing a beat on the electronic blood fest.

Bailey stood, jaw hanging open for a full minute, her eyes moving back and forth from her brothers and their rampage, to her uncle and his calm acceptance of it. Finally, she found her voice, "You really don't see a problem with this?" she indicated the pair with an open palm.

Staring at her through the narrow window that connected the kitchen to the living area, her guardian blinked at her for a moment. Finally he shook his head, "No, I don't have a problem with it. They're boys, Bailey; guts and gore comes naturally, an' the sooner they get tough the better off they'll be."

Glancing back at the pair seated on the floor, she managed to close her mouth, making a disgusted sound as she did, "Mom and dad would be furious if they knew this was happening."

"Well, like we discussed last night, your mom and dad are gone," Peter went back to preparing his batter. "It's just us now; we're the family, an' that means we go by what I think's best. I don't believe it's gonna hurt them, an' you need t' back me up on this."

"Back you up?" she glared at him, "I may not be able to do anything about it, but I'm damn sure not going to *back you up*." Storming back to her room, she slammed the door behind her; *son of a bitch. I can't believe that he's actually allowing them to play that shit. Wait, allow isn't the word, he's encouraging it!*

Moving to the bathroom a short time later, the girl put on her makeup and styled her hair. Still sulking, she made her way to the kitchen and helped herself to what remained of the pancakes, taking care to sit with her back to the television. Her hunger satisfied, she returned to her room to finish some schoolwork until time to head across the street for her shift at the shop.

Exiting the apartment, she heard her uncle call out to her, "Remember, straight there and straight home!"

"Yes, I know," she replied tartly, closing the door harder than necessary.

Bailey arrived at work with only a few minutes to spare, and felt relieved to see that Caleb was not seated in the dining area; at least not yet. Back in the office, she put her purse away and straightened herself, noting the dark marks on her face were fairly visible when you looked at her squarely. Inhaling deeply, she steeled herself for the comments she felt sure she would receive during the night.

Out front, she took her place at the register, and began taking orders. Deep down, she felt glad that she had proven exceptional at running the device, as cleaning the lobby had been a boring job at best, and meant that she would have been stuck where Caleb would have easy access to her if he wanted it.

Her thoughts fell to the young blond between customers, and her anger at him grew. *He could have told me he was my keeper; neglecting to do so was a lie, plain and simple.* Trying to force herself to think about other things, she quickly realized there was no good news in her life, and hadn't been in a while.

At almost seven-thirty, the man in question made his appearance. Stepping up to the counter, he had a fair amount of grime on his face, and his shirt covered in some kind of light colored powder.

"What will you have?" she asked curtly.

"Hi!" he smiled, showing his clean white teeth, "I

trust you've had a better day than me!" he laughed loudly.

"No, I haven't," she spat angrily, "I know who you are, so you can wipe that stupid grin off your face and give me your order."

His smile slowly faded, and he spoke more gruffly, "I'll take a cheeseburger, with the works, and an extra-large fry; an' make it a combo."

"Yes, sir; twelve-seventy-six," she held out her hand for his card. Swiping it, she handed it back to him along with his cup, "You're number five-nineteen. Go sit down!"

Caleb pursed his lips at her surliness, his own blood beginning to boil. "Sure thing, princess," he pointed a finger at her, "But be sure t' come an' see me when you get your break." Walking away, his shoulders drooped, and he filled his cup while glaring at her openly. Tossing the book on the table, he flipped through the pages to find his place, and began reading.

"Asshole," Bailey muttered under her breath while rolling her eyes.

The next guy in line looked around in shock, pointing at himself with an extended thumb, "You talkin' to me?"

"No, sir," she perked up, taking his order and smoothing things over.

At eight o'clock, she was given her break, and gathered her dinner. Standing with her tray in hand, she slid her tongue around inside her cheek, considering eating in the office to avoid him. Deciding to tackle the issue head on, she stomped into the lobby and plunked down on the leather bench facing him.

"You're a real son of a bitch, you know that?" she hissed. "And what the hell're you doing still reading that stupid book? I told you, I know who you are, and I know why you're here. You can quit acting like you belong."

Calmly closing the text, the man across from her clenched his jaw, causing the muscles in his neck to bulge slightly. "Le's get one thing straight, princess. I really do have a job here, and I am takin' a class. So, I will read whatever the fuck I want. I'm tired! I've had a long, hard day; jus' like yesterday, jus' like tomorrow's gonna be. The last thing I'm gonna do is sit here an' take shit from you!"

Bailey's mouth fell open, aware that she had never had anyone speak to her that way before. Even last night, when her uncle was angry, he had been more respectful. "You can't leave," she replied more calmly. "Uncle Pete says you're here to look after me or keep tabs on me, or some crap like that."

"Yeah," he nodded, folding his hands in front of him, "I am. My dad sent me, so I took the job to make some money while you're in school. You know, to contribute to the community."

"What community!" she flung her hands up and looked around, "You're not from here, so who cares if you work here or not?"

"Not... this one," he managed through gritted teeth, then leaned back in the seat and ran his hand through his hair, only making it worse. "I need a shower," he continued more calmly.

"Yes, you do. You're a mess," she frowned, "Why didn't you go get one before you came in here?"

"Because I was afraid if I went home, I wouldn't make it back over here, alright?" his voice sounded strained, still filled with raw emotion, "Look. Bailey," he flopped forward, leaning on the table, "Neither one o' us're callin' the shots here. Between your uncle an' my old man, we're jus' th' pawns. Fightin' ain't gonna do either of us any good."

Glancing at her plate, he flicked his fingers at it, "You should eat. Your break's gonna be over before you can finish."

Lifting a strip of chicken, the girl reluctantly complied. Watching her, Caleb's anger began to subside, and he knew he needed to have his say. "I really am sorry about your parents. I know losing them was hard."

Bailey cut her eyes up at him while continuing to eat, hoping to finish before she had to return to the front. Turning to look out the window, Caleb watched the lights on the street for a moment, then pushed on. "I'm not really your babysitter, or jailer. They're worried about you; they didn't want you gettin' into any trouble."

Finished with the meal, the girl wiped her face on one

of the brown paper napkins from the rack, "That's why you followed me and Ked?"

"Yeah," he nodded, stabbing the table with a stiff index finger, "An' that means they was right. You did need lookin' after. So we should call a truce, an' make the best of it."

"No, thanks," she retorted, getting to her feet and taking her trash with her.

Returning his hand to his hair, Caleb sat for a moment, then made his way to the bathroom to try and remove at least some of the dirt from his arms and face. Back at his table, he gathered his things, preparing to wait outside for the remaining few minutes before he walked his charge home. Beyond the exit, the cool spring air felt refreshing, and he leaned against the wall for what turned out to be a short wait.

When Bailey came out the door, she headed to the light with long strides. Catching up to her, Caleb caught her arm and spun her around to face him. "Ok, if this is how it's gonna be, I wanna make one thing clear."

"What's that?" her green eyes sparkled like embers beneath the street lamps.

"You wanted a friend," his nostrils flared as he spoke.

"Friends don't lie and keep secrets from each other," she lifted her chin bitterly, yanking her arm free.

"That's a child's view o' the world. You better grow

up, princess, 'cause nothin' is black an' white!'"

Bailey stomped her foot and wrinkled her nose, "*Why* do you keep calling me Princess?"

"Because you are," he half sneered, "You grew up with rich parents in a big house, an' you reek o' money an' privilege. But you're in a different world now, an' all that shit is *gone*."

Her brow furrowed at his emphasis of the word *gone*, but he ploughed on. "If you wanna make it here; make it in Lawson… you better get yourself together. There ain't no place for the weak, an' ain't nobody gonna carry your ass. You'll either get with the program, or you'll get left in the cold."

"Lawson?" she demanded, crossing her arms.

"That's where we live. That's our community. It's where your uncle's been takin' the boys, to get them acclimated. You're the one no one's sure about. An' like I said, you better get your shit together," his voice had dropped to a low growl, and he glanced down at her slender frame, "That's all I can say. That, an' we can be friends if you want. An' if you don't, then fuck off. Light's green," he pointed, indicating that it was time to go.

WALK THE LINE

Bailey climbed the stairs slowly, Caleb's words turning in her mind. They hadn't spoken to one another since he had told her to *fuck off*, and that was fine with her. Reaching the top, she turned towards the end of the balcony and the door to the apartment. Glancing down, she could see he stood, arms folded across his chest, waiting for her to go inside.

Letting herself in, she wasn't surprised to find her uncle once again sitting half naked in his favorite spot. Thankfully, he didn't speak when she entered, and allowed her to go to her room in peace. Closing the portal behind her, she noticed that her hands had begun to tremble, partly out of anger, but mostly out of fear.

Glaring down at the Dewitt phone, she knew she had one chance to save herself and her brothers. Lifting it, she quickly flipped through her list of contacts. Reaching over to ensure the door was locked, she moved to the far side of the room, putting her back into the corner and sliding down the wall beside her ironing board. Biting the side of her thumb, she listened to the ring.

"Nanna?" her voice cracked when the call connected. "Nanna! It's me, Bailey!" She sobbed loudly, clutching the phone and pressing it against her ear.

"Bailey? What time is it?" the voice on the other end sounded groggy, and the girl could tell she had woken the older woman.

"It's late, Nanna," she sniffed loudly, "But I had to call. We need your help."

"My help? What's happened? Where's your uncle?"

"He's here," she took a ragged breath, "Something's wrong though, Nanna. He had some guy watching me. He told me things tonight; something about some other town, where they're going to take us. And he's letting the boys play horrible games, and teaching them how to kill people."

"How to kill people!?! Good lord, Bailey, would you stop blubbering and start making sense? Let me speak to Peter; right now!" The older woman's voice had become shrill.

"I can't," Bailey wiped at the tears, "You have to believe me! Something isn't right here! We need you to come and get us and take us home!"

At that moment, her bedroom door swung wide, and her uncle swept into the room, butter knife in hand. Easily locating the girl in her semi-hidden position, he snatched the phone from her hand, glancing down at the screen. Lifting the device to his ear, he said simply, "Hello, mother."

Bailey couldn't hear what her grandmother said, but his expression remained calm, "Yes, I know it's late. I'm sorry. She's just upset. Don't worry; I'll take care of it." Ending the call, he stared down at the black screen for a moment before offering it to her. "You're stuck here, Bailey-girl. My mother doesn't want you there. Believe me, I tried to convince her to let you stay. Do you wanna finish this school year?"

The girl stared up at him, brushing her auburn hair out of her eyes, "What do you mean, do I want to finish school this year?"

"We're going to The Ranch. Soon. If you wanna finish this year, you better'd walk the line." His hand stiff, he pointed the tips of his fingers at her sharply, "If I have any more trouble outta you, we'll leave, an' you won't get the chance t' finish the year. You got that?"

Bailey gaped at him, terror causing her chest to heave, "And what if I don't *walk the line*? Do you think you can force me to do what you want?"

The grin spread slowly across his face, and her eyes dropped to stare at the salt and pepper curls that covered his muscular chest. She wasn't sure what she had expected him to say, but the fact that he left the room without saying anything, closing the door quietly behind him, scared her more than any words he could have spoken.

After a fitful night of sleep, Bailey awoke early the next morning and stared at the ceiling for several minutes. Taking her clothes into the bathroom, she had a hot shower and prepared for the day. She thought her world had been turned upside down when her parents died; *I guess that was only the beginning,* she sulked.

Grabbing her purse and backpack, she sat them on the end of the couch and joined Peter in the kitchen. Seeing the usual eggs, bacon and toast, she took her seat on the far side of the table facing him, and remained quiet.

Setting the dish in front of her, her guardian grabbed his own and a cup of coffee. Maintaining the silence, the pair cleaned their plates. Leaving her to deal with the dishes, he went to get the boys dressed for school. Half an hour later, they were ready to leave, and made their way down the stairs and into the parking lot.

During the drive, Bailey considered what Ked might think of her missing the bus. Of course, he should be in class, and she briefly wondered how he would react to her presence. Exhaling a loud sigh, she tried not to let it bother her, as there wasn't really anything she could do beyond muddle through, and stay out of trouble, as her uncle had demanded.

Glancing over her left shoulder, she could see Jase sitting behind the driver's seat, watching the traffic out his window and bouncing his feet merrily. Still considering her options, she quickly realized that she could get away alone, if she wanted to run. *He said he tried to get Nanna to keep me. He really doesn't want me here, so if I ran, he'd probably let me go.*

Returning her glare to the concrete that rushed by outside, she wondered if she could live with that choice. *If I leave them with him, who knows what'll happen to them.* The vehicle stopped in front of the elementary school, and the boys made a hasty exit, calling their goodbyes.

Pressing her hand to the glass, a wave of sadness threatened to bring her to tears. She and the boys had never been close. Bailey had been too wrapped up in her own life to worry about her little brothers; or her parents for that matter. Her mother had told her, not long ago, how proud she felt of the girl and her level of maturity; like a little adult, poised and ready to take on the world. *I miss you, mom,* her thoughts ran in circles.

Peter eased the SUV to the curb, and the girl pulled herself together. With a loud sigh, she grabbed the handle to exit and closed the door with a loud thud. Climbing the steps to the main entrance of her own building, she swung her backpack and purse around behind her, her uncle's words stuck in her mind; *why the hell am I fighting to finish the year? I could dump all this shit; but if I do, he wins. Besides, I can't let the boys down like that; they need me to look out for them.*

Inside, she made her way to her first class, a frown

etched on her delicate features. Taking her seat, she nervously shuffled papers, waiting for it to begin. Fortunately, when Ked arrived, he ignored her, hiding behind his shades and not giving her a second glance during that or their next class together.

The morning like slow torture, the realization came that she would have to eat lunch on campus. She wore a small pout into the cafeteria while she collected her tray and chose an empty table. She had never been inside it, and it surprised her that it actually held booths and tables, much like a restaurant, or at least most of the accommodations were.

Picking at her Chicken Alfredo, she nibbled at the creamy noodles until Ked flopped down on the chair next to hers, giving her a loud, "Hey."

Looking up at him with wide eyes, she stammered, "What're you doing?" Casting a glance at the rest of the room, she hoped that there were no other spies about, and she whispered loudly, "I can't talk to you. Or be seen with you. You have to go!"

"Why? Because of our little scuffle the other night?"

Looking at him head on for the first time, she gasped, "Oh my God! Did Caleb do that to you?" His left eye severely bruised and swollen, he had scrape marks along his cheek beneath it. His wounds had been covered earlier in the day by his dark glasses, which he flicked at her.

"Yeah, he did. I's really surprised you didn't call the

cops, neither."

"No, I didn't see any point in hashing through everything with them, as it is clearly over, and surely won't happen again," she continued to peer around her anxiously.

His eyes following hers, he queried, "What're you lookin' for?"

"To see if anyone's watching us," she whispered. "I'm in trouble, and I'm not allowed to talk to you. I really wish you'd go."

He snickered, "And here I thought things were going so well, playing hard to get this morning, after your friend jumped me. Maybe I should give you a little warning."

He leaned closer to her, ready to have his say, but she interrupted him, her voice a little too loud, "You're the one who needs the warning, *Ked*. The guy who jumped you is some kind of wacko and my uncle is messed up in some weird shit. Stay away from me, if you know what's good for you."

"Your uncle? What about your dad?"

"My dad is dead, Ked. My parents were hit by a semi back home a few weeks ago. Their car was crushed and went over a cliff." She inhaled deeply, her lip beginning to tremble, "And I think my uncle may have had something to do with it."

The boy stared at her, shocked by her accusation,

"You think your uncle murdered your parents? Why would he do that?"

"So he could have my little brothers," she breathed, "He was all set to bring them here. He knows way too much about them; what they like and how to gain their trust. We haven't seen him in seven years! A new car, a new apartment, with all new stuff. Something's not right, Ked. And he threatened to pull me out of school if I don't *walk the line*," she mocked her guardian's voice. "He wants to take us to his real home, at the ranch." She paused, a single tear trickling down her cheek, "And he doesn't even want me. No one does."

"You don't say," Ked stared at her, slack jawed for a moment, "You have any idea how crazy that sounds?"

"Yes, I do," she wiped at her cheek, "That's why I'm not telling anyone. That's why you have to stay away from me. I'm scared of what they'll do if you don't, and not just to me... or you," her green eyes pleaded with him.

"I get it," he shifted on his seat, "Ok then, I'll leave you alone an' not talk to you anymore." He chuckled, "I've been told to beat it by lots of girls, an' I can take it. But that's gotta be the most insane excuse anyone's ever used to get rid of me." He laughed as he walked away, finding another group to join, and leaving her without a second thought.

WISH IN ONE HAND

Bailey walked on eggshells for the entire week. She had been a social creature before her parents died, but that was another life. Presently, she only wanted to survive, getting by on her own the best she could.

Her uncle rarely spoke to her, but she often felt as if he were watching her. Her distrust of him and his motives smoldered, and she spent many hours thinking about the accident and how things had fallen into place. And of course Caleb still came into the shop every night when she worked, and escorted her home. He didn't talk to her either.

She knew that protesting would likely have a negative result, so she accepted her invisible chains. Choosing to focus on her studies, she made top marks, and found that between work and school she at least had plenty to keep her busy. From the outside, she felt certain that everything appeared perfectly normal. On the inside, she felt empty and alone.

On Friday, she arrived home to find a moving van parked at the bottom of their stairs, and two men in blue shirts were carrying boxes up to the apartment. Taking the steps in twos, she raced to the top to see if all of her personal items had indeed been sent to her. Standing in the doorway of her room, her lip stuck out in disgust when she realized none of the furniture had been sent, and only half at best of her clothes had been forwarded.

Opening boxes, she pulled out shirts, pants, and dresses to begin hanging and folding them. Her night off from the store, she would have everything in its place before bed if she were diligent. Surveying the closet, finally filled with familiar things, she sighed deeply, feeling a duality of emotion she had come to accept. *You know how the saying goes,* she admonished herself, *you can wish in one hand... and you know what you can do in the other.*

Choosing not to wallow in her discomfort, Bailey picked up her Dewitt phone, and began scrolling through her old friends list. She had several hundred, but as the names and icons rolled by, she quickly realized there wasn't a single one she could message and explain her situation to; none who wouldn't think her a raving lunatic. Not one she could call, and expect anything but disbelief at her tale.

Allowing a deep sigh to escape her, she tossed the device back onto the nightstand. She didn't bother to even look at the Mason phone, as she had only a dozen contacts on that profile, and the only one she would be remotely comfortable messaging would be Ked. He had already laughed in her face, so she saw no point in going any further.

Crossing the hall, Bailey took a shower and dressed for bed. Waiting to fall asleep, she realized they actually only had four weeks left in the school year, and her uncle would take them to his ranch. Glaring at the ceiling, she wondered if he would bring her back for next year, or if he would register them wherever it is that they were going.

Lawson; that's what Caleb had called it. So it must be a town, and therefore have a school. So why didn't he take us there to begin with? Why move here and let us settle in, only to uproot us for a second time? Bailey found she still had more questions than answers, and she was growing tired of not knowing.

Of course, asking her uncle those questions would likely bring nothing but problems. But one other person knew the answers as well; someone who hadn't spoken to her since their fight. Turning to face the wall, she ran her fingers across her left cheek. Thinking about the young man who had saved her, she wondered if he could be trusted.

He said we were both stuck; as if he wasn't happy with their situation either. *Maybe building a friendship with him could be useful after all.* Staring at the painted surface before falling asleep, she became resolved to give it another try, starting at the burger shop on her next shift.

The following evening, as she prepared to go in to work, Bailey could feel a twinge of nervous energy. She intended to speak to Caleb; to forge ahead with their relationship, in a strictly platonic sense of the word. The sensation of butterflies in her gut disturbed her, and she told herself firmly that it was *not* romantic interest that put them there.

What put her on edge were the secrets that he held. He had hinted at the dark undertones that lay within Peter and his friend's motives, and she knew that this young man could give her details about their plans. *The trick will be getting him to share.*

Arriving at the shop, her day began as usual, and she took her place at the register with an almost giddy feeling; joy at the comfort that familiarity offered. Dealing with the steady traffic kept her mind busy, and soon her target arrived, causing her to break into a wide smile of greeting.

Caleb froze upon seeing it. Turning to look over his shoulder in an exaggerated fashion, he found no one behind him. "Well, you're in a good mood tonight," he quipped, not really expecting her to reply.

"Yes, I am," she cast her eyes away from him, unable to remove the grin, "Would you mind if I visited you during my break?"

He stared at her, stunned for a moment and wondering what the little minx was up to. With a small shrug, he nodded his approval and gave her his order. Leaving the counter, he pursed his lips, curious, as she clearly could not to be trusted based upon past performance.

Rushing to gather her dinner when the time came, she hurried out to her seat in the booth with her new confidant. Closing his book, Caleb took a long drink from his straw, waiting for her to open the conversation and reveal her motives. Glancing out the window, he could see the streetlights had come on, and the sun had almost set.

"Thanks for letting me sit with you," she said sweetly, a bit out of breath.

"No problem," he replied calmly. "I tol' you we could be friends."

"Yes, I know," she nodded, then took a large bite of her burger and washed it down with a swig of coke.

"So whadda you want, Bailey?"

Her eyes flitted up to stare at the forwardness of his question. "Am I that transparent?" she smiled coyly.

"Yeah; we haven't had a conversation in what, over a week? Now you wanna talk, so what's up?"

"I want you to tell me about Lawson," she pasted on a bright smile. "My uncle says he's taking us there when school is out, and I want to hear all about it."

"He told you he was taking you to... Lawson?" Caleb's expression became perplexed.

"Well, the ranch; isn't that the same thing?"

"No," Caleb shook his head, fidgeting with the paper wrapper from his straw, "It's really not." Inhaling deeply, he returned his gaze to the window for a moment, then looked her square in the eye. "The Ranch is your uncle's house; his barn, the horses, those things. Lawson is," he shrugged, "The community; the people. Each has a different role. The buildings are important, but the people are even more so."

Bailey felt the warm tingle creeping up her spine; the one that told her she was close to getting what she wanted, if she were patient. "Right, that's what I want to know about," she encouraged him, "What are the people like? What will it be like to live there?"

Pursing his lips, Caleb wasn't ready to reveal what he knew, and felt fairly certain she wasn't ready to hear about the small township in the middle of the desert, either; not the truth at any rate. "It's nice," he said simply. "They're hard-working people, with a common goal. If you take their way o' life t' heart, you won' ever leave."

She stared at him blankly, his words not really meshing with his ominous warning from the week before. "Wow," she breathed, "I can't wait to meet them." Her break over, she stood to get back to work. *But at least we're on good terms again,* she consoled herself. *That means eventually, he'll tell me what I want to know.*

Walking beside him a short while later, covering the

familiar path that led to her new home, she decided to take a different approach, "So, what is it that you do during the day? What job can make a man so dirty?"

"I drive a concrete truck," he answered flatly, "An' yeah, it's nasty business." He grinned, shoving his hands in his pockets and watching the ground as they walked.

She smiled, aware that his tone had changed slightly, and they paused at the bottom of her stairs, "And where do you stay, if it's not as comfortable as all of this?" she indicated the complex with an open palm.

"I rented a small camper in a trailer park on th' other side o' town. Everyone is there on a weekly basis, like a motel; mostly men, who come an' go with the work," he explained.

"You're right, that doesn't sound very inviting," she mumbled.

"No, it ain't. It has a small bed an' a shower that you can sit on the toilet while you use it." Something about the description gave the girl the giggles, causing him to laugh for a moment himself. "Anyways, trying t' do anything in a space barely big enough to turn around in is frustrating."

"I bet you'll be glad to get back to Lawson yourself, then."

"Yeah," he nodded, straightening in preparation to leave, "I guess that I will."

"This really is a strange place," she sighed, happy

that she had gained a small amount of trust. "Goodnight, Caleb," she gave him a little wave, making her ascent.

"Goodnight, Bailey," he called a soft reply before turning and making his way back to his ride, and the long drive home.

NO WAY OUT

The days passed quickly, with everyone around her in a buzz about the coming summer break and their future plans. Bailey, however, felt more trapped with each passing day. The realization that she had virtually no way out of the life that lay before her weighed heavily in her thoughts. Her uncle called the shots, and she had no choice but to follow his command.

On a Saturday morning, only a few weeks before their summer was to begin, the head of the household made an unwelcome announcement at breakfast. "I'm gonna invite Caleb to move in with us. He can stay on the couch until we're ready to leave town," he stated matter-of-factly, while watching her face morph into a stunned expression.

"You can't do that!" she protested, "There's barely enough room for us as it is!"

"I can, an' I am," he chuckled at her, "More people

live in less space all over the world; it's time you learned to share. Besides, it's only a couple o' weeks, an' we'll be headed to The Ranch."

Staring at him with a cold green glare, she knew it would be pointless to continue the debate. *What he says goes,* she mocked him mentally, dropping her protest with a heavy pout.

That afternoon, Caleb arrived on a motorcycle, which he parked next to Pete's Suburban. It surprised her to discover that's how he got around, as she had pictured him owning an old, beat-up pickup or something of that nature.

The bike was a large model, with two oversized saddle bags, and a bitch seat between them. The boys were excited by his arrival, and made requests over dinner to be carted around and given rides. However, Caleb quickly drew the line, "Sorry, guys; you'll jus' have t' wait until we get back to The Ranch, an' you can ride the four-wheelers again. I really wouldn't feel right cartin' you around."

Bailey had never been up close to one before, much less ridden on one, and she agreed with a toss of her waves, "That's right. You boys have no business on such an unsafe contraption."

Her expression shifted to pure shock when Caleb laughed a rebuttal, his blue orbs sparkling, "Well, I wouldn' say the same t' you, little bit. I'd give you a ride any time."

"Not here," Pete interjected. "You can do all that when we get home."

Caleb continued to eat, unabashed by having to wait, "Yeah, that's true; we can wait, an' we'll have plenty o' time." His smile wide, he genuinely hoped she would accept the offer.

Something about his grin made the girl's stomach lurch. She had been playing nice for the last two weeks, but so far he hadn't divulged anything new about their destination, or anything else for that matter. The high handed manner of both men bothered her, as they seemed to believe she should, or would, simply follow their commands without question or explanation.

"What if I don't want to ride your stupid bike?" she quipped angrily. "You know, you guys do an awful lot of assuming."

The two men stared at her, Caleb pausing in mid bite, "It was just a suggestion, little bit."

Bailey cringed, the use of his new pet name aggravating. "In case you haven't noticed, I don't like it when Uncle Pete calls me *Bailey-girl,* and I sure as hell don't like being called *little bit.* My name is Bailey. Use it." Standing, she scraped the remainder of her food into the trash and stomped down the hall to her room, closing the door with a slam.

Peter chuckled, watching the two boys clean their plates, "She's a fiery little thing. That auburn hair really suits her."

"Yeah, it does!" Caleb agreed with a smirk.

"You think you can handle her?" the older man cut his eyes over at him, toying with his fork.

"Yeah; I got it covered," Caleb leaned back in his chair, also watching the two youngsters. "We're gettin' along good. When the time comes, she'll fall in line."

"I hope so," Pete took another bite, allowing the conversation to drop.

In her room, Bailey sat on the edge of her bed, rocking back and forth. It was her night off, but she wished she had a shift, and an excuse to be out of the house. As soon as dinner ended, they would be in the living room, gathered around the wide screen television. She had watched them a few times, and hated to see her uncle giving the boys pointers at how to be better at killing people, even if they were only pretending through the game.

Turning to stretch out on top of the covers, she stared at the ceiling, with her arms folded behind her head. *I guess we really are leaving soon; and Caleb being here does make more sense, since he walks me home every night.* Still, the idea of his being under the same roof bothered her, with the vibe she picked from him often making her uncomfortable.

We're friends, she rationalized; *at least he thinks we are.* Deep down, she resented him almost as much as she did her uncle, and held on to her anger. *Yeah, he can think that all he wants,* her chest rose and fell calmly. *I know the truth. I damn sure won't hesitate to get me and my brothers out of this mess; all I need is the opportunity.*

The last day of school arrived all too quickly, and Bailey could feel the tension growing within her. The next morning, her uncle handed her a single box to pack her things.

"Take only your warm weather clothing; everyday kinda stuff," he instructed. "Leave the rest for next year."

Well, I guess that means he does intend to come back, she sighed to herself. Placing the carton on the floor, she tied her long hair up in a ponytail, and set to work choosing exactly the items that she would want. Caleb had said there were horses, and the boys had described a very rustic location, so she figured that jeans were in order. Also deciding on a few pairs of shorts, she found about a dozen shirts, in varied sleeve lengths and thicknesses, and tossed them all in.

It's also a desert area, she recalled, *so I may need a few heavier items in case the evenings aren't warm enough for my liking.* Grabbing a hoodie and a sweatshirt, she packed them as well. Finally, she located the pair of hiking boots that her grandmother had sent. They had been in her closet back home, and she had only worn them once, on a field trip with her science class.

Removing them from their smaller box, she packed them on top of the clothes, and filled in the empty spots with all the socks, bras, and panties that she could locate.

Taping the flaps shut, she sat on the edge of the bed and stared at the brown cardboard, a frown wrinkling her forehead.

The last time I moved, I was too young to remember it. Now I've moved twice in less than three months. Of course, if they were coming back to the apartment for the next school year, this wasn't really a move, and would be more like an extended vacation. *Like a summer home.* She hoped so at least, and had asked Mark, her boss, to hold her job for her until she got back, to which he had agreed.

The thought brought a small smile briefly to her lips. Glancing up, she discovered Caleb stood in the hall, watching her through the crack in the door. Pretending she hadn't noticed, her smile faded, and she moved to begin placing her grooming items into her suitcase. Opening the door to clear out the bathroom as well, she feigned surprise, "Hey, Caleb."

"Hi," he beamed, his mood seeming much lighter in the last few days, "You all set?"

"Almost," she didn't return the grin. "I'm a little on edge about where we're going. Uncle Peter still hasn't said much, and you aren't any help, either."

"You're gonna be fine," he reassured. "I'm not being secretive; I jus' don' know what else t' say." He leaned on the door frame, watching her gather bottles and jars from a drawer and toss them in a bag. "You probably aren't gonna need any o' that stuff," he commented in an offhanded manner.

Cutting her eyes over at him, her features drew into a deeper frown, but her hands continued to move. "I never go without my makeup," she retorted. "Not since I was twelve years old."

The mention of her age caused a stunned expression to cross his rugged features. "Oh, hell," he gasped, "Did we forget your birthday?"

"Yes," she sighed, "It was two days ago." She had been a little depressed that no one had mentioned it, but wasn't about to point it out herself.

"Wow, so you're seventeen. Almost legal," he chuckled as if it were a joke.

Turning her back to him, her hands began to tremble, her female intuition working overtime. "Yeah, whatever."

"I'll remember it next year," he promised, watching her from behind.

"I don't plan on knowing you next year," she quipped, unable to catch her angry thoughts before they spewed out of her mouth.

Caleb only laughed at her, "Yeah, if you say so, little bit." Resisting the urge to smack her rear, he turned around and left her to her packing. Instead, he made his way to the boys' room, where they were helping their uncle gather their things.

"You two all set?" he called loudly, ready to chip in

wherever needed. The twins had really taken to him, as they had their uncle, and it made him smile to see them so eager to get to their new home. "You guys know my little brother, right?"

Stopping to have a conversation with their new friend, Jess placed his hands on his hips, "You mean that kid with the red hair?"

"Yeah, Carson. He's my little brother." Carson Cross was twelve years old, and therefore close enough to be a good playmate for the twins. Of course, he had been raised on The Ranch, so he held a bit more familiarity with the way of life, which would be useful as the twins were assimilated.

"We taking anything from the kitchen?" the tall blond asked calmly.

"Nah, just leave it; we can throw the food items that won't keep away." Pete shook his head. "We get the clothes an' the blankets from the beds. Everything else can stay. Oh, an' we can take the TV with the PS4."

"Roger that!" Caleb gave him a mock salute, and went to find trash bags to pack the bedding, tossing them in a pile by the door when ready. Looking around, he decided to pack the gaming system, and placed a few of the disc cases in the box with it. Doing a bit of mental calculation, he realized it would be a tight squeeze, getting everything to fit in the Suburban.

"I guess that about covers it," he called to the older man, who joined him in the front room with one of the boxes.

"Yup, we're set. Get it in the car an' we're ready t' roll."

With everyone helping to carry the haul down the stairs, it didn't take long and they were loaded to depart. Stopping long enough for a good meal before they left town, the group piled into the overstuffed vehicle and left Midland with the intention of return in the fall. Deep down, Bailey wondered if that would actually happen; after all, nothing else in her life seemed to be going according to plan.

HOME ON THE RANGE

The twins watched a movie, falling asleep a short time after they left. Taking the highway west for a while, they soon turned off and headed south. Looking over her shoulder, Bailey could see the boys, resting in the seat behind, with their belongings piled in the last row and the cargo area beyond. She couldn't see Caleb, bringing up the rear, but she knew he was there. Almost as if she could feel his presence, her resentment of the tall blond smoldered.

Turning back to watch the scenery drifting by, she frowned at the recollection of her first Google search of the area. She had discovered that it was desert like, with hardly any plants to speak of, and no animals, save an occasional bird, to be seen. "This is a terrible place," she muttered under her breath.

"Why's that?" her uncle asked softly.

Cutting her eyes over at him, she continued to hold

the scowl in place, "Because it's in the middle of nowhere. No people, nothing. Only empty, open... nothing." She slouched in her seat, her body expressing the depths of her despair.

"It's not so bad. Besides, some people like being away from the crowds," he kept his eyes on the road as he spoke. "Brenda and I worked really hard on this place, for nearly twenty years. If she hadn't gotten sick, we still would be."

"The boys said there are other people out here; on the ranch."

"Yeah," he nodded slightly, "There's a few families that live out here. We form a community, or a township, if you will."

"Let me guess, called Lawson," she completed for him.

"Lawson?" his eyes grew wide, "Who said anything about Lawson?"

Bailey bit her lip, his tone taking her by surprise, "Caleb mentioned it; then he wouldn't give me any details. Isn't that where we're going?"

"No," Peter strained to glare at the bike he could see in his side mirror, rolling along behind them. "We're not going to Lawson. We're going to The Ranch. That's the name of our little town; *The* Ranch."

Running her tongue over her teeth, the girl finally made the connection, "Oh my God. How stupid of me.

The Ranch is really a name, like Midland."

"Yes," her uncle nodded. "Don't take it so hard. I can see how it would be confusing." He grinned at her, glancing in her direction for a moment. "I want things to work out for you here, Bailey-girl. I really do. Just give it a chance, ok?"

Rolling her eyes, she turned back to her window, "Whatever, man. I'm stuck here, as you pointed out, but that don't mean I always will be."

A couple of hours passed, the pair sitting in silence, until the sun had moved over into late afternoon. She could see a small building ahead long before they got to it and her uncle began to slow down when they were close. "What are you doing?" she demanded, still unhappy with the man behind the wheel.

"We need fuel," he supplied. "The trip is just a little too long for one tank of gas, so we have to fill up." Climbing out at the tiny store that had no other buildings around it, he closed the door gently behind him.

Twisting in her seat to look behind her, Bailey could hear their voices outside. Leaning over into his seat, she could see that Caleb had joined him on the other side of the pumps, and was filling his bike as well. She scowled at the pair, the sound of their laughter only causing her displeasure to worsen; *assholes*. Sitting up straight in her seat, she ignored her uncle when he rejoined her.

Leaving the station behind them, the group continued south for another long stretch, until they reached their turn. Easing across a rough cattle guard and onto a smaller road, which hardly qualified as two lanes with no center stripe, they put the sun at their backs. The land on either side of the narrow band of pavement appeared as barren as all the rest she had seen on their journey. However, off in the distance, Bailey could see the faint outline of trees with a backdrop of hills.

Ten minutes later, she could make out their destination more clearly; there were indeed green limbs branching up into the sky, partially hidden from view by a large wall. To her dismay, The Ranch appeared to be behind the massive structure that extended at least half a mile along the front, with the road ending abruptly at the enormous gate, obviously intended to keep people out.

Leaning out the window, Peter typed in his code at the keypad, and the entrance rolled open, allowing them inside. Bailey's heart had begun to thump loudly in her ears, and she fought desperately to keep her breathing under control; *it's a prison!* In the back of her mind, she had held on to the belief that she would have an opportunity to get away, and take her brothers with her.

Seeing their final destination unfolding before her, she became grief stricken, realizing it had been an impossible dream. Twisting in her seat, she couldn't see the gate roll shut, but she heard the clang, its echo heartbreaking.

Inside the compound, they passed through a small group of large turbines, seemingly used to generate electricity from wind power. To her right, she could make out a small airstrip, which ran down the far wall of the complex. Turning to her left, large buildings lay beyond, but their purpose not ascertainable.

The vehicle rolled slowly along, allowing her to take everything in, and she noticed that there were a few house like structures, and perhaps a diner, followed by another small group of windmills. She also noted there was a labyrinth of smaller dirt roads, crisscrossing the area and leading away from the main road to the far reaches of the resort.

Finally, Uncle Pete made a left-hand turn onto one of the smaller thoroughfares, and she could see that the far end of the compound lay maybe another seven or eight hundred feet down the paved access. Passing between a small grove of trees and a large greenhouse, they pulled up in front of a garage.

A large house lay to their right, bigger than any that Bailey had ever been inside, but certainly not the largest she had ever seen. "Is this yours?" she managed to ask, somewhat in awe. She had always thought of her uncle as destitute, but this was not the home of a poor man.

"Yeah," he shrugged, with a nod, "This is my place. Brenda an' I built it, thinkin' we would fill it with kids; didn't work out that way, though. Her folks are here, looking after things for me, since I had to go an' take care of you guys. There's some other guys, too, but we'll worry about them later."

Bailey frowned at the thought of his keeping things from her, feeling more vulnerable than ever. Waking her brothers, they went inside to use the bathroom, and then began unloading their belongings. Hauling everything into the living room, they dropped it all in a large pile, to be distributed later.

At that point she noticed Caleb was no longer with them. "Where'd he go?" she asked, trying not to appear that it mattered.

"He went home," Jess surmised, "His house is down the street," he pointed in the direction from which they had come.

"You play with his little brother, what's his name," she frowned, unsure what to make of their new surroundings.

"Yeah, he's neat. He's got a three-oh-eight and promised to teach us how to use his twenty-two!" Jase tossed out lightly.

"What's a three-oh-eight?" she asked anxiously, afraid that she knew, but didn't want to believe it.

"Knock it off, you guys," Peter interceded, "We'll get to all that later. Right now, we need to get all this stuff hauled upstairs. Bailey, your room is on the third floor, end of the hallway, overlooking the east side of the property." Handing her the box she had packed that morning, he dismissed her from the group.

Trudging to the stairs, and focusing on her footing, she made it to the top a bit out of breath. Sure enough, a plain room lay at the end of the hall, containing a double sized bed and large dresser that hugged the wall between the entrance and the closet. The bed stuck out into the room, with a window at the foot, a second on the far side, and a small desk in the corner between them.

Placing her box on the bare mattress, she worked her way around to the far side, discovering the path around her bed to be about three feet all the way around. *Damn, it's cramped; and again, no bathroom.* Through the wide open frame, she could hear the squeak of a windmill turning in the breeze.

Leaning out the opening to survey the area, she noted that a patch of green grass and a line of trees lay beneath her, running between the structure and the noisy machine. She also noticed that the walls enclosing the compound came to a corner about a hundred and fifty yards from the house, beyond the windmill. However, the closest portion stood only about twenty yards to the left of her other window.

"Here's your sheets and a bedspread," an older woman entered without knocking, leaving the articles beside the box.

Bailey stared after her, surprised she had come and gone without so much as an introduction. Heading back down the stairs to locate and retrieve the rest of her things, she felt angry to find that her brothers' room had been located on the second floor. "Why do they get to be there and I'm all the way up at the top?" she inquired curtly.

"Because, there isn't room for you on this floor," her guardian informed her shortly. "You'll be fine up there, an' I'm sure you'll enjoy the privacy."

Grabbing her suitcase and the trash bag that held her bedding, she frowned, *I hate this place.* She had already noticed the stark simplicity of the furnishings; almost as if she had walked onto the set of an old western. "Is that why you brought the TV? Because there isn't one here?"

"Something like that," he retorted easily, grabbing more of the boys' things and following them up the stairs. "We'll eat in about an hour. Until then, you get to make yourself at home."

Carrying the rest of her gear up to her quarters, she noticed that each floor held a single bathroom; *great, looks like we get to share,* and she scowled at the claw footed tub on her way by. She paused as she passed the other two bedrooms on her floor as well, observing that they both appeared to be occupied, with each containing a set of twin beds and a desk facing a single window between each; *like dorm rooms. So, at least four more people live in the house; I can't wait to meet them.*

Making up her bed and getting her belongings lined out, Bailey eventually made her way to the stairs, ready to go down for dinner. Running her hand along the old wooden banister, she wondered how long the house had been there, as everything seemed to be a mixed lot; an odd blend of old and new. *Guess I'll find out soon enough,* she sighed as she located the dining room to join the others.

NEW GIRL IN TOWN

Bailey entered the dining room slowly, a quiet chaos whirling around her. Her brothers were seated at the table, on the side closest to her, along with her uncle at the head of the long wooden surface. On the far side sat a large black man, another man who looked to be of some oriental descent, and a much older gentleman with shining silver hair.

The woman with the sheets and blankets busily placed pans on the table, and the group of males began serving their plates. Sliding quietly into a seat next to one of her brothers so that she faced the old man, the girl breathed deeply, trying to make heads or tails of the strange scene before her. Unexpectedly, two more men came in and filled plates, exiting through the far door that led into the kitchen.

"Who the hell *are* all these people?" Bailey blurted her eyes wide.

SAMANTHA JACOBEY

"Friends; family," her uncle spoke, his mouth full of food before he swallowed it. "You'll do good to keep your trap shut an' your eyes open, little bit."

She grimaced, displeased that the older man had taken to using her new nickname versus the old one; not an improvement in her estimation. Scowling at the dishes, she prepared her plate and began to eat, discovering that the meal tasted much better than it appeared. The gathering spoke little, leaving the boys to make up much of the noise that filled the room. As soon as the pair was finished, they pushed back their seats, eager to have a bit of time outside before bed.

Left alone with the adults, Bailey lay her fork across her empty plate, "So, do I at least get an introduction?"

After a moment of silence, the black man showed her the pink palm of his right hand in a small wave, "Devon McWilliams."

She nodded slightly, then shifted her gaze to the gentleman to his left.

"Nung Ceu," he tilted his head towards her.

"Hi," she exhaled through her nose loudly. "I'm Bailey." She looked at the older, silver-haired man across from her.

"James Fox; call me Jim," his teeth clicked when he spoke, "This's ma wife, Connie," he indicated the woman at the end of the table.

Her eyes shifting between the faces, she mumbled,

"See? That wasn't so hard, now was it?"

The woman cleared her throat loudly and stood, gathering plates to take them to the kitchen. Following suit, Bailey lifted her own, and those of her brothers, carrying them through the doorway. Continuing the process, the girl helped the woman clean up after the meal, and put the utensils away, while thinking to herself, *this is the maid's job,* but suspecting they didn't have one.

While they worked, Bailey could hear the men talking in hushed voices before they moved outside. A short time later, her brothers came in, stomping up the stairs and headed to their bath. Her uncle trod behind, herding them on their way and tucking them into their beds shortly thereafter.

She followed the sound of their giggles, locating their room on the second floor. Making her way inside under the pretense of bidding them goodnight, she was shocked to find their space had once again been fully stocked for their arrival.

"Wow," she breathed, "Pretty neat stuff you have here," her eyes slid easily across the bunk-beds they had crawled into, and the bookcase that took up an entire wall, its shelves packed with books and boy-toys. "Was all this here the first time you came?" she queried nonchalantly.

"Sure was!" Jess provided eagerly, "All for us," he added with pride.

Her gaze fell upon their guardian, who tucked a boy in the bottom bed, then giving Jase a pat on the back in the top. "You guys sleep well. We have a busy day tomorrow." He smiled at them, and the trio seemed perfectly happy, with or without the frowning female in the room.

Moving out into the hall, Bailey waited for her uncle to exit. She leaned on the banister and stared down at her trembling hands, the living area on the first floor below them. When he came out to stand beside her, she could feel the fear seize her lungs, and she could not bring herself to ask the questions that burned inside her mind. Instead, she simply bade him good night and took the stairs to the third floor.

Gathering her night clothes, she made her way to the bathroom for a quick shower. Prepared for bed, she returned to her room, locking her door before she stretched out on top of her covers. Lying in the darkness, she listened to the screech and whine of the windmill outside her window, her mind filled with dark and harrowing thoughts and ideas.

This was no ordinary ranch and these were no ordinary people. She knew that they had not wanted her there; her reception had been cold and most unwelcoming. Their behavior towards her felt odd, setting off little alarm bells in the back of her mind, and for the first time, the thought occurred to her; *I may not make it out of here alive.*

The following morning, Bailey awoke early to the sound of boots on hard wood. Her eyes opened wide, staring about at the ceiling above; her heart raced, certain they were right outside her door. After a moment, the pair of footwear ambled down the hall, and she tossed back her covers. Springing out of bed, she dressed hurriedly before making her way to the bathroom to pee and put on her makeup.

Finally decent, she made her way downstairs, where the rest of the house and then some were busy consuming breakfast. She noted Caleb's presence, along with a boy with fiery red hair; his younger brother Carson, she presumed. The middle-aged couple was more than likely their parents, as the woman looked very much like the two boys.

As soon as the meal had been consumed, all of the men disappeared, taking the boys with them while leaving Bailey with the women. Once the dishes had been washed and put away, Martha Cross offered her name, and instructed the girl to follow her so they could get started on the garden before the heat of the day.

Reluctantly, the girl followed, and they crossed the dirt path to arrive at a large nursery filled with young plants. Passing through the structure, the field in back of it turned out to be a solid acre square. She had scarcely noticed the rows from her window the afternoon before, but standing in the midst of them took her breath away.

Martha handed her a set of hand tools, and led her

over to a row of green beans. Instructing her how to clear out the weeds without damaging the crop, she put the girl to work.

Bailey obediently threw herself into the task, unsure if or how she would challenge the authoritative way the round woman who stood a few inches shorter than her spoke. Martha simply assumed her directions would be followed, and so they would be.

Working diligently, sweat began to drip from her face and brow. Swiping across it, Bailey noticed that much of her makeup wound up on her arm. She looked around to discover that the field had become dotted with a handful of other women, all wearing straw hats and stooped over, working on various areas of vegetation.

Martha observed the auburn haired beauty from the shade of the building a short time later. She knew that the girl wasn't supposed to be there; it had been discussed several times at *meeting*, and it had been a consensus that she did not, nor would she ever, belong. And yet, here she was, kneeling down in their field, digging up weeds. Reaching over, she lifted a spare hat off of its nail next to the door and carried it out to her, along with a jug of water.

"Here," she stated in monotone, "Broughtcha surprise." She offered the items, watching the girl stand, and noting the red flush to her face.

Bailey accepted the hat, using her long fingers to smooth her hair and the covering to hold it in place.

Taking the jug, she hoisted it and chugged a copious amount before returning the lid. "How long do we do this?" she demanded, less afraid of the woman who appeared to be in charge.

"'Til lunch," Martha replied crisply. "Few more hours," she grinned, turning to make her way across the field and check on the progress of the rest of that morning's workers.

Bailey watched her picking her way through the rows, grateful for the cover that eased the heat and glare of the sun. Returning to her knees, she observed her palms that had already become raw from the rub of the tools against them. Taking up her tiny fork and spade, she worked her way down the line. When she reached the end, she looked back to discover that another girl followed behind, picking up the foliage that she had uprooted, and placing it in a bucket.

When the sun shone straight down upon them, Martha stood in the shade of the long structure, calling loudly to the scattered group. Each gardener gathered her tools and made her way to the front for a brief gathering, where she introduced the newcomer to the others. "Bailey, these are the Burns and the Smalls."

Going down the line, their names rolled easily off her tongue; Lacy Burns and her daughters, Amber and Rebecca, who all three had ebony colored hair, with bottomless brown eyes and deeply tanned skin. The other three, Deanna Small and her daughters Alexya and

Kimber, had fair skin, which they kept well covered in the blistering heat.

Bailey observed that the latter three also had pale blue eyes and hair that went from medium brown on the oldest, to lighter brown, and eventually to honey blond on the youngest. The group was not overly welcoming, but at least polite, and the girl felt glad she had not thrown a fit about being made to work in the field. She gave them a weak smile, grateful when they dismissed her to return to her residence to freshen up before lunch.

Trudging up the stairs a few minutes later, Bailey couldn't think of a time she had ever worked so hard. Making it to the bathroom, she glared into the mirror in disgust. Her makeup appeared severely smeared and outright missing across large portions of her face. *No wonder Caleb said I wouldn't need it,* she grumbled to herself before she washed off the remainder of it.

The water and soap stung her fresh blisters, and she bit her trembling lip while she dried them. Flexing her digits a few times, she allowed a few tears before she wiped them away, unwilling to let the people around her see her suffering. Her features set firmly, she exited the cubicle and made her way to the kitchen, where the meal had been prepared.

Once again, Connie placed dishes on the long flat surface in the dining room, and the men seemed to materialize out of thin air. This time, the boys were served plates at the kitchen table so that the two men

Bailey had not previously met could join them. Glancing down the row, she only had to wonder for a moment who they might be before they introduced themselves.

The one seated immediately to her left grinned broadly. "Hi, I'm Luis Montez," he announced with a sparkle in his mahogany colored eyes.

The man next to him grunted, "Don Finch," without bothering to look up from his plate.

Bailey felt out of place, listening to them discuss their day's progress, as well as the chores they would be tackling in the afternoon. She had never imagined people who lived or worked as hard as these appeared to, and she felt a bit forlorn in the midst of them.

Still not sure how or why they had chosen such a life, she pondered her new situation, having many questions and few answers at the moment. However, being the new girl in town, she had decided to take her uncle's advice, keeping her mouth shut and her ears open, and hoping she would figure things out.

JEALOUS MUCH?

After her first day in the field, it became obvious that Bailey Dewitt was Martha's charge. Whatever the woman worked on, the girl gave a hand, and she did so without argument. The structures she had seen the day she arrived turned out to be barns and pens, where horses and farm animals were housed, and although she did not work inside with the animals, she did learn how to process them into food.

They slaughtered a large hog the second day after she arrived and she spent one full day and several afternoons at the diner learning how to prepare the meat for curing into hams, pickling it, or canning it for long term storage. The stench of the blood hung in the air, and she felt sick at the sight of chunks of flesh tumbling out of the grinder for sausage. In the end, she had been grateful she had not been present for the actual butchering of the carcass.

The woman gave the girl directions matter-of-factly, staring at her while she worked with almost beady brown eyes. Bailey noted that she did not hold idle conversation with her, and appeared uninterested in learning anything about her previous life. Another woman from town came in to help, bringing her daughters, but they too refrained from making idle chit chat.

Instead, the women watched a large screen television that hung on the back wall of the dining room, listening to the news from the outside. Bailey had discovered it to be the only one in the community, other than the one they had brought for the games, and it never displayed anything else. During the processing of the hog, she began to make a better connection between the lives of the people who surrounded her, and the beliefs that they held most dear.

The initial incident occurred the morning of the fourth day, when a large volcano in Baja erupted, sending the small group of women into a mild frenzy. Word spread quickly through the small community, and Bailey could see the genuine concern on everyone's face while they ate their lunch. Laughing at the group to herself, she found the idea amusing; *what, do they think one little volcano is going to destroy us?*

She allowed the question to percolate in her thoughts, but refrained from asking it aloud, as she had become accustomed to gathering her information about the group by observation only. *These people are nuts,* she snickered at them under her breath, but as their virtual prisoner, it seemed wise to keep the impression to herself.

That afternoon, while helping in the diner with the hog, Bailey saw and heard the broadcasts, and began to feel a bit of fear herself. Shocked by what the media was putting out, she began to see the situation more clearly. *With this as their only window to the world, their view of society is so bleak; so distorted.*

Constantly feeding on the dark stories that bring ratings has made them overly sensitive. Things that the rest of humanity saw as normal were blown out of proportion on The Ranch. *Of course, it's not entirely their fault; they need a better source of information and a bit of balance, that's all,* she rationalized. This realization did nothing to improve her opinion of the community as a whole, and she went to bed that night with much to ponder.

Her routine in place, the girl awoke with the sun each day, and ate her breakfast with her brothers and the rest of the household. She then worked in the field until lunch, followed by helping in the diner for the afternoon, and most evenings.

Bailey resented the amount of time and energy that they asked of her, but did so in silence. She could see that no more was asked of her than any of the others, and to complain would have been rude in the least, and perhaps dangerous in the midst of the social order she could see coming into focus around her. By the end of the first week, she had fallen into obedient submission, in awe of what actually took place at The Ranch.

The evening on the seventh day, she was finally allowed time to herself, and she took advantage of the few hours alone. Having been curious since her arrival, the girl traversed the entire circumference of the small township. Following the massive twelve-foot brick wall, she appreciated the fresh air after her chores in the cramped and odor filled space where they prepared the food.

Making a trek around the dirt paths that crisscrossed the landscape, she wryly considered how it brought new meaning to the term *gated community*. Measuring it off by counting the bricks, she determined the barrier ran about twenty-five hundred feet east to west, and fifteen hundred north to south; in essence, the place was huge.

While she made her way back to the ranch house, she noted that the two small turbine groups held six total, and that all of their electricity came from wind power. In addition, there were three water wells, with windmills atop them, so the water tower stayed stocked by local resources as well. She stared up at them in fascination, wondering if there was in fact anything that they needed from the outside world.

Silently eating her dinner while surrounded by her housemates, she considered the plethora of trees scattered across the grounds. One area, next to the diner, held what they generally referred to as the orchard, but fruit trees could be found anywhere that shade was desirable.

She had discovered more than a few dozen fruit

bearing trees, including a variety of types, lying next to buildings and along the pathways. A group of grape vines grew in one corner of the compound, and a pair of massive pecan trees stood one at each end of the horse arena and feed barn. Many of these had been planted when her Uncle Pete and Aunt Brenda first began working on the property over twenty years ago.

Creating a mental tally of what she observed, the girl presumed that the group had become completely self-sufficient, as the food being produced was easily more than they were consuming. In the end, she calculated that the amount stored in the cabinets of the ranch house and the other family dwellings to only be a small part of what actually existed; in essence, they were hiding it somewhere and she secretly wondered why.

Secretly, because she had no intention of asking what became of the rest. She had quickly determined that no one had much to say to her, and she grasped the concept that they viewed her as an outsider. She would have to prove her worth among the group as Caleb had said, or she wouldn't be welcome, and none appeared too eager to get to know her.

Her brothers swept away to their baths, Bailey made her way up to her room and stretched out across her bed to listen to the quiet and the moan of the giant machine outside. *I've only been here a few days, but it feels so much longer,* she lamented. *How in the hell do these people do it?* Exhausted, she allowed her eyes to close and fell asleep before she could have her own shower for the night.

Her days continued to pass in a similar manner, doing whatever chore was presented to her, always trying to keep her chin up about the forced labor. She also watched for ways and things that she might use to her advantage, but so far had been unsuccessful. She wanted to take her brothers and leave, but how she could accomplish that feat had still not presented itself. Even her cell phones refused to work, getting no signal, and she almost felt as if they had become lost to the outside world.

The second week of their internment ended with the boys' tenth birthday, and a huge celebration took place at the diner. For the first time, Bailey was able to observe the entire community gathered at one place at the same time, thirty three members total counting herself and her siblings.

During the party, she met Allen and Paula Knight with their two daughters, followed by William and Katherine Tate with their two daughters. As they were introduced, a strange realization settled over her.

Making her way through the rest of the guests, she greeted the younger woman who had helped with the hog, and her two daughters, and the odd observation solidified and leapt to the front of her mind; *holy shit, they're all girls!* The idea took her breath away, and she swung her gaze once more, taking a mental head count. *Yup; ten young women and girls, and only two boys,*

Caleb and Carson. With the addition of Jess and Jase, the numbers were still severely lopsided.

Pinching her lip nervously, she could feel a lump in the pit of her gut. *No wonder my uncle didn't want me.* They had more than enough females, and what they really needed were more boys. The idea gave her a sick feeling, since she had thought before that their delivery into her uncle's care had been suspicious.

But could he really have had something to do with mom and dad's crash? The thought terrified her, and of course she had no proof; however the more she learned, the stronger the possibility seemed. Choosing a seat away from the others, the girl ate alone, allowing her mind to ponder her new discovery undisturbed.

When the meal had been completed, and all of the adults had settled into smaller groups for games and conversation, Bailey decided to have another look around. Leaving the central seating area, she made her way out through the glass doors and onto the covered patio, her mind racing.

At the far end, on the last table of the row, the older group of the young people had gathered, and seemed to be having a meeting of sorts, which Caleb appeared to be in charge of. However, as soon as Bailey approached, a silence settled over them, and they only stared at the newcomer as if she was grotesquely deformed and they had been struck speechless.

Raising her hand in a small wave, "Hi, guys," she

managed in a small voice, with a tiny grin to back it up.

Amanda Knight, a tall girl at five-foot eleven-inches, tossed her long blond curls over her shoulder and quipped, "I think you're in th' wrong group. The kid's table's over there," she wafted her hand at the other end of the patio, where the younger crowd had gathered to check out the boys' new toys and gifts.

Raising her chin, Bailey countered, "Sorry, I'm not a child," which brought a round of snickers from the rest of the young adults.

"Oh yeah? I guess you need t' prove that, then," she issued her challenge without hesitation.

"'Manda, stop it," Caleb bit sharply, glancing between them.

"Make me," she shot back, still sneering at the girl's auburn locks. "Le's get outta here; head over t' th' stables fur a bit."

"Ok," Bailey instantly agreed, not even sure what would be in store once they got there, but unwilling to appear weak in the eyes of her new nemesis. She noted that Caleb slowly shook his head at her, but she felt unwilling to alter the plan, and followed the young people sedately.

Exiting through the front of the diner, the group ambled along the asphalt, all the way to the main gate. The entourage laughed and joked with one another as they moved, and Bailey could tell they were good friends, probably having known each other for years, if not all their lives.

Taking the dirt path that ran between the barn and wall, their pace seemed unrushed, and she began to feel more relaxed in their midst, with an odd desire to be accepted by them. She noticed that the tallest girl had quite a muscular build, and could easily have become a model with her gorgeous features and long golden waves. Back home, she would have been just the sort of girl Bailey would have hung out with, being the cream of the crop and perfect cheerleader material, even with the attitude.

Arriving at the stables, she had thought they would follow the curve and move around to the canopy and corral, but instead, they continued into the grass behind the row of stalls and scattered about beneath one of the trees. Dropping onto the ground, the gathering created a large circle, striking relaxed poses in the shade of the largest of the three.

Leaning against the trunk, Caleb assumed the position of leader, his harem spread out before him. Moving to take her place next to him, Bailey felt determined to fit in.

In the blink of an eye, the tall blonde snatched a handful of auburn hair and yanked her back, "Where the fuck ya think yur goin'?" She released her, allowing her to stand straight, awaiting her explanation.

"Excuse you," the girl rubbed her tender scalp, aware she had never been in a physical fight with anyone in her life, not counting Ked.

"Ah no, you don' sit by him. In fact, you go sit over in th' pig's stall," she raised her hand to indicate the long barn and pens they had recently passed.

"What the hell's the matter with you?" Bailey demanded loudly, drawing herself up to her full height and squaring off with the young woman. Remaining about two inches short of matching the local, she refused to back down, "Are you jealous or something?"

"Jealous my ass," the other girl flew into a rage at her obstinate attitude, lurching forward and knocking the smaller girl to the ground. Sitting on her belly, she began to beat her in the face, her knuckles skinned and burning where she punched her while the rest of the girls watched in surprise.

Bailey could hear Caleb's deeper voice screaming Amanda's name, and a moment later the girl had been removed from her chest. Rolling over, she buried her face in her hands, sobbing at the blood that covered her fingers. She felt the warm sticky ooze coating them, and her body trembled at the rush of adrenaline that coursed through her veins.

At his urging, the collection of gawkers moved on, taking her attacker with them. Once the area had cleared, he rested his hand on her back and knelt down beside her. "Here, little bit, come on. Lemme see," he pulled at her shoulder, trying to maneuver her and get a look at the damage.

Reluctantly, she obeyed, sitting back on her heels with her toes pressed into the ground beneath her. Peering up at him, a stream of blood ran from her forehead into her eye, and he immediately pressed a thumb against it, applying pressure to the gaping wound, "Well, fuck." He held her there for a moment, then bade her to follow, pulling her to her feet.

On the wall of the barn, he located the spigot and opened it up enough to get a good flow. "Come on, le's give it a wash so we can see how bad it is."

Kneeling on the uphill side, Bailey laid her face into the cascade, washing away the blood for a few minutes. Blinking, she could see the tainted water creep slowly across the brown soil, creating a large, dark puddle. Raising her chin, her teeth chattering lightly, she allowed him to inspect the damage. Watching his furrowed brow, she realized the prognosis wouldn't be good.

"I think you need stitches," he finally muttered.

"Why'd she do that?" the girl queried, on the verge of more tears.

"You were right, she's a bit jealous. Thinks we need t' get back together, but that ain' hapnin'." He pulled off his shirt and rolled it, "Here, hold this against it," he guided her hands to position them. "That's it... keep it snug."

"She's your girlfriend?" Bailey breathed, finding her feet when he grasped her arms and lifted her.

"She was. Not anymore; not in over a year," he

released her and cut off the valve. "Kathy's the nurse; come on an' we'll get her t' fix you up."

Making their way back to the diner, Bailey waited outside, holding the cloth firmly to her forehead while Caleb located the woman in charge of medical in the community. Large tears stained her cheeks once more when he returned, which only made him feel worse than he already did. Dropping an arm across her shoulders, he held her against his bare chest, and the pair followed the nurse to her small office located in the southeast corner of the compound, across from a windmill.

Once the girl sat on her table and lowered the rag, Kathy made her assessment. "So, what happened here?" she asked nonchalantly.

"I fell," Bailey stated immediately, while Caleb glared at her in surprise.

The older woman shifted her eyes to the girl, then over to the young man, waiting for a truthful response; she could easily see her patient had been in a fight. When neither of them made any effort to change the story, she shrugged, "Ok," emitting an exaggerated sigh.

Fifteen minutes later, the pair exited the small room, a bandage covering the row of stitches for the moment. "You'll need t' pull that off so air can get t' them, but you wanna keep it clean," Caleb informed her as they strolled up the sandy path. Arriving at his house, which lay at the intersection where the dirt road met the pavement, but on the opposite side, he pointed it out for her, "This's our place."

"Yes, I figured that out," she smiled slightly as they took the next minor thoroughfare that ran beside the water tower and led to the ranch house. "How long have you guys been here?" she asked in a quiet voice, still unsure if she really wanted to expose her curiosity. Glancing at him, she noted his features did not appear angry at her prying, seeming almost eager to share with her.

"All my life," he replied with a grin. "My dad an' mom started building this as soon as he was out o' the military, an' I was born the same year the house was finished. Your uncle moved th' house the Knights live in out here a couple o' years later, an' he an' Brenda lived in it until the ranch house was finished an' the Foxes joined us."

"You knew my aunt?" she squinted at him, as the sunset hung behind his wide shoulders and glistened on his golden skin.

"Yeah, I did. She was a real nice lady." He paused, having arrived at the veranda that covered two sides of her current residence, "I'm really sorry, Bailey. She had no right to attack you."

"It's ok," the girl faltered, toying with the bloody shirt she still carried, "I've never been in a fight before. Not really sure that getting beat up even qualifies," she snickered. "But, I've managed to do it twice since I met you."

"Yeah, well, you need to learn," he pushed his hands away from his body, indicating there was no argument with what he suggested.

"Learn what?" she lifted her chin and swallowed, her gaze flickering across his muscles to look him in the eye.

"How to fight. How to defend yourself. You don' wanna live the rest o' your life bein' helpless, do you?" his words smacked of disdain.

"I'm not helpless!" she quipped in a loud voice, "And I don't need to be insulted after the day I've had!"

"Well, you need somethin'," he replied, "'Manda's tough, an' I warned you; you'll either get with the program or you'll never make it here." Turning abruptly, he called over his shoulder, "Keep the shirt." Ending the conversation, he headed back towards his own home, eager to get away from her before he said anything he might actually regret.

HEADS OR TAILS

Peter Mason eyed the cut on his niece's forehead angrily the following morning. "Care to explain that?" he gripped his fork tightly, using it to point at the fresh wound.

"I fell," Bailey stuck to her story.

"Fell? On what, a fuckin' flight o' stairs?" his face grew red at her dishonesty.

Bailey stared at her plate, pushing her scrambled eggs around nervously, "You shouldn't talk that way in front of the boys," she mumbled.

"Don't change the fuckin' subject!" he smacked the table with a clenched fist, causing the youngsters and the Foxes to all jump at the rattle of the dishes.

Rising to pick up their plates, Connie took the boys into the kitchen and set them up at the smaller table, out of the way should the disagreement in the dining room escalate. Returning to her seat at the opposite end of long flat surface, she stared calmly at Pete, waiting to see how he would handle the girl's deceitfulness.

"I'm not gonna ask you again," he made a subtle threat.

"I got in a fight, ok?" the girl didn't look at him.

"With whom?" his anger evident, Peter enunciated each word clearly. When she failed to respond, he demanded, "Did Caleb do that to you?"

Bailey's face shot up, her jaw dropped slightly, "No, he didn't! Look," her eyes darted away for an instant, "Why do you keep thinking he would hurt me? He wouldn't, ok?" *He's been nothing but nice to me,* she admitted to herself with a fixed jaw.

Her uncle returned to his food, taking several large bites and allowing his blood pressure to return to normal. After the lengthy pause, he tried again, "I just wanna know what happened."

"One of the girls jumped me," Bailey confessed in a small voice. "Nobody likes me here, and she said I couldn't sit with them. She told me to go sit with the pigs." She heard Jim snort loudly, suppressing a laugh, and she shifted her gaze over to him.

The old man stared at her, "Ain't s' tough, are ya?"

The girl shook her head slowly, "No. I wasn't raised to fight with people."

He chuckled loudly, "Well, I figure you'll learn. An' the sooner th' better."

Peter pushed his empty plate back, placing his elbows on the table and folding his hands together in front of his face. "We need t' have a meeting."

"We've had enough meetings," Connie cut in. "We all said our piece. You need t' take it to heart, Peter Mason; get this girl outta here while you still can." Rising abruptly, she gathered the empty platters and headed to the kitchen to begin the day's chores.

Bailey stared after her, curious at her words, while feeling somewhat vindicated. *I've known in my gut since we got here that I wasn't safe.* "What did she mean by that?" she asked quietly, speaking to the two men who remained in the room with her.

The pair exchanged a long, silent stare, before returning their attention to her. "What she means is, you're right. Most of the community is against you staying here," Pete confessed in a much lower voice. "It's not you, ok?" He offered a brief justification, "They've all worked really hard to build what we have…" The old man grunted, and the explanation trailed away.

"We gotta lot at stake here," the silver haired gent took over, "An' don' nobody wanna lose it due to an outsider."

"What about the boys?" she demanded sharply, fear gripping her that they could be harmed.

Her uncle exhaled loudly, "They're different," he confessed, "They're younger, an' can still become a seamless part o' the community. You, on the other hand, are older. Less likely you can learn what you need to know. An' then there's the trust issue..." His voice disappeared again, his conflict evident on his face.

"I see," she sat up straighter. Her lip quivered slightly, "So what is it that you guys have been working so hard for; what're you so afraid of losing?" Her face crinkled, her own anger breaking through.

The men shared another glance, and the old man answered calmly, "The end o' the world. When it comes, only th' strong survives, an' nothin' the rest o' the world's doin' right now's gonna matter."

Bailey's jaw dropped as she recalled their reaction to the volcano eruption, and she stared with wide eyes; *were they serious about that?* "The end of the world? Are you people crazy?" she gasped, unable to keep the shock out of her voice. *Maybe they're more than hypersensitive; maybe they really believe it!*

"No, we're not crazy," her uncle answered directly, "The end is comin', an' we intend to be ready for it. I know most people agree with us on some level, but what they lack is the conviction to do anything about it. We've been working for twenty years to prepare. We're ready, one way or the other."

"Is that why you wanted the boys?" she asked breathlessly, unsure how he would react to her hinted accusation, and unable to make heads or tails of their insane notions.

"I never had any kids. But my sister did, an' I'm left

with hers, if that's what you mean by *wanted*," Peter stated calmly, hoping to reach the girl with some words of wisdom and to diffuse her animosity. "I'm responsible for you; an' the boys."

"You don't have to take care of us. I can get a job and support us – we don't need you," Bailey shot back crisply, driven by the desire to grab her siblings and run.

His eyes burned into her, the air passing over his lips making an odd hissing sound. Taking in his shifting features, she could feel the tightening in her gut, and she laid her fork on the table to hide her trembling digits.

"You don't need me? Like you're gonna take care of a pair o' ten year old boys all by yourself! You're seventeen years old, Bailey; you got your whole life ahead of you. The last thing you need to do is throw it all away on a foolish plan such as that," he berated, his words cutting deeply.

"What the hell do you mean *my whole life ahead of me*? Why don't you make up your mind?" she fumed, "One minute you're telling me our world is going to end and we have nothing to live for and the next you make it sound like I'm stupid for wanting to be responsible!" She tossed her head, refusing to let fear dissuade her from making her case.

"We plan so we're ready, but we can't quit livin' our lives, the ones we have now. Yeah, our world is gonna end. It's inevitable that the human race'll one day fall away," the veins were visible in his neck as he spoke.

"An' I plan on bein' one of the ones that makes it. But it may not be in my lifetime. Or yours. We don' get t' know that part. All we know is, it's comin', an' we need to be ready."

"Then you take care of the boys, and I'll go," she pouted slightly as she made the suggestion. "They're boys after all. They'll like the things you want us to learn, but I don't need this... any of this." She glanced unconsciously at her healing blisters, able to admit she had no real desire to be a part of the community or its efforts.

"You don't need it right this minute, but when the shit hits the fan, you're gonna need it to survive," he countered smoothly.

"Isn't that what you have all that food stashed away for? So you can survive?" she quipped, not having seen the stockpiles, but aware that they were there, somewhere hidden away.

Pete's jaw dropped slightly at her casual mention of his hard work and years of preparation, "I don't ever wanna hear you say another damn thing about what's stashed away, you got that? There's people that would take it away from us, by force if necessary, when the time comes that we need it." He waited for her slow nod before he continued to chastise her.

"As far as what I want you to learn, it's the thing that'll ensure your survival, not the stores. They only get us a year or so, if we're lucky. It's what we know about how to provide for ourselves that'll determine if we make it or not," his eyes glittered as he finished. "Either way, you ain't leavin'. Your parents are dead, an' that means your well-being falls t' me. It's my job to look out for you, an' that's exactly what I'm gonna do."

Bailey cut her eyes over at the old man, who had listened to the exchange in silence, his deep green eyes evaluating what each of them had said. Dropping to gaze at his fleshy lips, she wondered where he stood on the issue. "Is that how you see things? If I'm not wanted here... Why would you make me stay?"

The old man didn't respond, his eyes cutting over at the other man for a moment before he stood. His face grim, he shuffled across the floor and exited through the front, headed to the door and the pathway beyond.

THE MEEK

Bailey could feel her blood run cold as she watched the back of the silver head disappear. Her heart beating wildly inside her chest, she shifted her gaze back to her relation, breathing in a deep pant. "You wouldn't hurt me, would you?" she asked in a timid voice, the fear of what lay in store holding her firmly in its grasp.

"No, Bailey-girl, I'd never hurt you," he replied calmly. "You know what the bible says?"

She stared at him blankly, having no clue what he was referring to.

"The bible says that *the meek shall inherit the earth;* but around here, that's a tough line to sell." Standing, he knocked on the table with a knuckle, "Use your time wisely, little bit. Learn what you can and hope that it'll be enough." He let the words hang in the air as he followed their patriarch out into the street.

Catching up to his father-in-law, he fell into step

beside him, "She needs time; that's all."

"You know as well as I do that ain' gonna sit well with the others."

"Yeah, but what's it gonna hurt? We can give her 'til the end of summer; we don't have to decide now. Or act now. Give her until the fall," Peter appealed for his niece.

"I'll mention it t' Bill; see if he'd be willin' t' wait. I can't guarantee it though," the old man cast a quick glance at his oldest daughter's husband. "You shoulda left her, Pete. If you really cared, that's what you woulda done."

"I couldn't do that. She already got herself in trouble, and there's not anyone else willing to look out for her," he bit angrily, thinking of his mother for a moment. "Just ask him. Tell him I would consider it a great favor to me; one I would owe him for." Making an abrupt turn, he headed into the stables, ready to be productive.

Back at the house, the girl sat at the table for several minutes, allowing their conversation to turn inside her mind. *They want the boys; I'm certain of that.* And she came as part of the package, but not a portion the locals seemed interested in having.

Rising from her chair, she cleared the few items that were left on the table and placed them on the kitchen counter to be washed. Returning with a cloth, she cleaned all the flat surfaces, her mind drifting to the days she spent in the dining room back at the burger shop. A wave of self-pity washed over her, recalling she had asked her manager to hold her job for her; she realized it had been a futile request.

"I'm not ever leaving this place," she muttered quietly to herself. Finished with the furnishings, she located the broom and dustpan and took care of the floor. Once the room was spotless, she let herself out the back door and surveyed the garden to her right. Seeing the hats dotting the field, she left the porch and made her way down the dirt path to join them.

Entering the greenhouse, she lifted her cover from the nail, twisting her hair, and using the bonnet to secure it out of her face. Staring blankly at the tools hanging from the peg-board for a moment, she selected a spade and fork, and made her way out into the morning sun. Finding a row that looked in need of tending, she knelt down and began to clear the debris from around the precious plants.

Martha noticed the young woman some time later, and stood watching her while using her hand to shade her eyes. Caleb had informed her of the altercation between his old sweetheart and the girl. Turning and putting herself into her work, she tried not to think about Pete's niece, or the fate that would soon be hers. The girl had become an issue within the small community; an issue that would sooner or later be resolved.

Shortly after the sun reached its peak above them, the group gathered their trash in buckets and carried them over to the compost bin. Lining up instruments and hats inside the shed, the girls chatted amicably to one another, leaving Bailey feeling left out. Following the group of friends, they arrived at the ranch house, where a large lunch had been prepared.

Taking a small plate of the food, Bailey noted that many of the others from the town came through and took plates as well, which she had learned to be the norm. Sitting off to the side alone, she finished her meal and washed her dishes. Putting them away, she slipped quietly out, taking the path that led between the arena and the back side of the diner.

Arriving at the animal barn, she made her way inside. Passing between the various pens and cages, she noted Amanda, along with one of the other girls, working at the far end. Backtracking, she left the way she came in, having no desire to speak to the tall blonde.

Making a left outside, she entered the canopy and then the stables, breathing a sigh of relief to find the man she hunted. "Hey," she spoke quietly when she stood beside him, reaching up to stroke the neck of the horse he appeared to be grooming.

"Hey," he replied with the hint of a smile. "You done with your chores?"

"Yes, we tended the garden today," she replied, glancing around to ensure they were alone. "I was hoping to ask you for a favor."

Caleb stopped his brushing, his hands still resting against the massive creature, "Ok, what kind o' favor?"

he inquired while he stared at her, a little afraid of what she might want.

"Will you teach me how to fight?" she asked timidly. "I know I said I didn't want to learn," she stammered, "But I think maybe I should."

Wiping at the sweat that trickled out of his blond spikes, the young man nodded, "Yeah, you should. Lemme finish here, an' I'll take you out back an' show you a few things. 'Course, you know you're not gonna learn it all in one day," he added, his hands once again stroking the horse.

"I know," her voice perked up a tiny bit, "But as often as you can, I would appreciate." Watching him for a few minutes, she grew bolder, "Have you eaten yet? Connie made a huge lunch, and it looked like most everyone had some."

"Yeah, we do it that way most times. More efficient to have one or two doin' the cooking for everyone, so the rest of us can work on other things." He cut his eyes over at her, still kneading the flesh before him, "An' no, I didn' get any."

"Ok, while you do this, I'll go grab your dinner," she smiled in earnest and exited quickly. Back at the ranch house a few minutes later, she peeked through the screen to survey the empty room. Slipping inside, she made a plate and covered it, then grabbed a glass of water and exited in a hurry. She did not believe anyone would mind her taking him a plate; *I'd simply rather not explain it,* she rationalized her sneaky demeanor.

Arriving at the stables, she met up with Caleb as he came out, and grinned when she presented it to him. "I got you some water, too."

"Thanks," he shot her a brief smile, taking the items and indicating for her to follow. Leading her around behind the building, they stretched out beneath the shade of the tree where she had taken a beating the day before, and he began to devour the delicious meal. Between bites, he inquired, "So, what changed your mind?"

Bailey wrinkled her nose for a moment, then answered softly, "I don't really know. I've just been thinking about things; what you said and all. I mean, what if you're right? What if I need to learn so I fit in better around here?"

He cut his eyes over at her, knowing she would never fit in with the tight-knit community. His mother had informed him last night what the elder members of the group intended to do with her. He had been sworn to secrecy, and felt sick to his stomach at the thought of what lay in store for the mild-mannered young woman. He wasn't sure heartbroken would be the word for it, but his emotions were torn to say the least.

Managing to finish the food, he laid the empty cup across the plate, all to be returned to the kitchen later. Little went to waste at The Ranch, and he smiled slightly at the idea of their frugalness.

Standing, he offered her a hand to her feet and began

instructing her, the way his father had done for him more than a decade before. "You know, my old man an' your uncle were marines together; they made sure we all got trained."

"Nope, I did not know that," she smiled, doing her best to follow his directions.

"Yeah, we learned about hand to hand encounters, an' how to shoot, too. We have a really cool gun range on the other end of the compound," he continued to enlighten her while they worked.

"Is that what's in that huge building," she nodded, "I wouldn't have guessed that. And the girls all learned, too?"

"Yeah, girls learned, too." He briefly wondered if they would be upset with what he taught her, but a short time later he dismissed the idea. As long as she lived on The Ranch, she would be a part of the community in his eyes, and it would only be right to do this for her. After a good hour of giving her the basics, he asked in a quiet tone, "You had enough?"

Bailey smiled up at him, feeling exhausted. She had been in pretty good shape, working out and performing with the pep squad. But that had been months ago, and she felt a little winded at the moment. "I guess I've gotten a little out of shape."

"Yeah, you need t' work on that, too. Maybe get up early and go for a run, or whatever it is that you do for exercise," he could immediately see the surprise skitter across her face, "An' no, working in th' field don't count. You gotta do something that gets your heart rate up. That's how you build stamina."

She nodded, pleased with his honest opinion, "Sure, I can do that. Anything else?"

"Just keep workin'; do what's asked o' you an' focus on what you can do t' contribute to the community. Tha's what it's all about here." He punched her in the shoulder playfully, "Take the stuff back t' the house, an' I'll see you later. Practice those moves, an' I'll give you another lesson tomorrow if I can."

Bending over to retrieve the tumbler and plate, she watched him head down the path and go into the barn. *I wonder if he's going to visit with amazon girl,* she allowed herself the derogatory name for the blonde who had beaten her.

Walking down the path, her thoughts churned, and she hoped that one day she would be good enough to even the score. *The meek may inherit the earth,* she kidded with herself, her hand reaching up briefly to pat her stitches, *but I'm tired of being meek. It's time I got tough, and that's exactly what I intend to do.*

LOVE THYSELF

Starting the next day, Bailey took the initiative and Caleb's advice to heart. She wanted to invest time in herself like she had never done before. Getting up early, she went for a run, and discovered that others in the group did so as well. Spying the four men who shared her floor in the ranch house, she followed them to the front of the med center, where she found herself in the midst of half the town, all gathered there in the cul-de-sac.

Caleb grinned at her as she came jogging up with the group of men, but the four girls who surrounded him did not look so pleased. Noting that Amanda stood to his right, Bailey felt fairly certain that the two of them were indeed a couple, *even if he wants to deny it*, and she refrained from getting any closer to avoid the confrontation.

"What're you up to, girl?" the tall black man named Devon interrupted her thoughts, seeming disturbed by her presence.

"I'm… having a workout. This isn't a private party, is it?" she gave him her best smile, and hoped they would allow her to join them.

"The weenie workout is in the evenin'," Amanda scoffed, eliciting a few snickers from her friends.

A silent look passed around the circle of men, and Luis' grin grew twisted as he ignored the other girl's jab, "Naw, little bit, you can join us."

Bailey picked up on his use of her dreaded nickname, but in light of trying to fit in, she chose to ignore it. "Thanks," she smiled more confidently, her stomach knotting a little in the process.

At that moment, Peter and the twins came into the light, the boys shrieking when Bailey popped into view. "Hey, are you gonna hang out with us today?" Jess appeared overjoyed, grasping at her for a hug.

"Hi guys," she glared with pretended joy, shocked that they would be there at such a young age, "Are you getting into shape, too?"

"We sure are!" Jase readily agreed, "We're gonna be big an' strong, just like the rest of the men folk!"

The girl felt mildly put out at his reference to the men of the group, surprised that the boys understood the division of the sexes that seemed prevalent there within the four walls of The Ranch; *more than likely someone is pushing that piece of propaganda on them.* "Me, too," she breathed, almost to herself, keeping her emotional state out of view.

Pulling her aside, Nung ushered the girl into the gym to fill her in on some of the particulars. Leading her through a normal door that stood about three feet from the outer wall closest to the med center, he pointed out the cubbies along the left hand wall.

"There," he indicated one of the spots, "That one's empty, so you can use it for your gear. Keep your water cup here, and anything else you need while you're at the gym. And there's the bathrooms, with a single shower in each on the back wall," he wafted a hand in that direction, "In case you ever need it."

He nodded, continuing with the tour to the right, guiding her through the rooms that held a variety of equipment. "Down in the center, you have your mats for aerobics and stuff like that, and there really is a workout that the older women have in the evenings in here. Yoga and stuff, if you decide you would like that better," he led her past the storage racks and pointed to the wall space. "Here we have the walls marked for height, in case you wanna throw the medicine balls against it."

She noticed the shelving that held a variety of sized balls, with different weights, plus the kettlebells and small dumbbells, all lined up neatly. "What's this for," she queried, indicating the wide roll up door, one of three she had seen from the outside. She had noticed the building before, and had assumed it to be another garage because of them.

"We got heat, but no cool," he grinned, "If it gets too

hot, we pop the door open to let some air in," he motioned towards the wide entrance that matched the ones in the next two sections of the building.

Turning back to the equipment, he continued when they entered the last section of the structure, "Here in this end, you got your bars, rings, and some boxes for climbing and jumping," they stopped to take it all in, "And at the far end you got your setup for lifting. All the bars are marked, either thirty-five or forty-five pounds, and these are the weights," he indicated the flexible discs that could withstand being dropped. "You ever been to a gym before?" he gave her thin physique a dubious glare.

"Well, yes and no," she admitted casually, "I was a cheerleader, so we worked out, but not like this."

"A cheerleader," Amanda scoffed from behind her, "That makes sense."

"Is there something wrong with that?" Bailey snapped, noting that the rest of the crowd had filed in behind them. "Having been here all your life, I wouldn't have thought you would even know what *cheerleader* meant." The air grew thick, the animosity hanging between them.

"Naw, not at all," she moved her taller frame closer to glare down at the girl while her voice dripped with honey, "I've been out a time or two, an' I've read enough t' know what that sort o' girl's all about."

"Well, nice t' see you two gettin' along," a booming voice cut into their volley of cloaked insults.

Bailey had not met John Cross formally, but she knew him from the other morning's breakfast and the few other social occasions. Everyone gathered around him as soon as he arrived, and the workout of the day began without preamble. She quickly learned that the members of the group took turns, planning what would be their routine, and it therefore changed, with pretty much something new every day.

John's day to lead, he briefly went over the agenda posted on the large chalkboard inside the first door. As soon as he had explained what they were doing, everyone went to work, moving at their own pace to complete as much of the assignment as possible.

Bailey made as many of the moves as she could, imitating the others, and being instructed from time to time by the few willing to help her. Watching the blonde covertly, she discovered that Amanda's highly muscular build was no accident. The young woman pushed herself as if she were one of the men, and the smaller girl felt in awe of her at the moment; *no wonder Caleb likes her.*

The group used a variety of cardio and weight-lifting exercises, as well as full-body movements that were designed to increase overall strength and flexibility. Bailey did her best to keep up, but she knew she would have to push herself just as hard if she ever wanted to be a part of the group. *If she can do it, I can do it,* she told herself firmly.

While she got the hang of things, she thought about

the routine that took place in the evenings; *older women, he said.* The women who met at sunset and enjoyed a lighter version, filled with yoga and aerobics only. *Tempting, but I can't allow myself to be delegated to the weenie portion of the group.*

"Nice to see you hanging in there," Nung informed her with a wide grin, then showed her improvements for her push-up technique before continuing, "You really can take your pick; no one is going to think less of you if this is too much."

Bailey grimaced, fairly certain that his statement held truth, and there would be little she could do that would make them think any less of her than they already did. *What I need are ways to make them like me more.*

By the time they were finished that morning, the girl had begun making a list of sorts in her mind. Well, two really, one being her list of friends in her new home; a rather short one indeed. She wasn't sure she would call the other list her enemies, but they were definitely less tolerant of her, and Amanda's name landed at the top.

Half joking, she labeled them the *naughty* and *nice* lists, thinking that the latter would be her go-to community members when she needed anything, and the former, the group she would do her best to avoid. Her putting things into perspective brought a smile to her lips as she arrived back at the ranch house, and climbed the stairs to her room. *If I'm careful, I just might survive here after all.*

MAID OF HONOR

"Bailey, can you take the cart an' fetch us a new bag o' flour?" Alissa Porter called from across the workbench in the diner's kitchen.

"Sure," she washed her hands and swished her auburn locks behind her. "I'll be back in a jiff."

From the very first day, it had been Bailey's job to help in the field with the gardening each morning, and that never changed. However, the rest of her chores had become haphazard since Martha had been providing less structure for her afternoons and evenings after her fight with Amanda. Left to her own devices, the girl gravitated towards two things; people on the nice list and opportunities to learn.

Sliding onto the cushioned seat, she wound around the dirt road, observing the sun as it sank lower in the sky; *I need to hurry. Everyone will be ready for dinner soon.* Pulling up behind the Tates' garage, she let herself into the cellar and bounced down the steps. Locating a sack of the white powder, she hauled it up and dropped it on the back seat of the repurposed golf cart; *there we go.*

Making the return trip, she recalled how much easier her choices had become once she had dedicated herself to working hard and doing her best to fit in. *I need to earn my place,* she reminded herself, *as Caleb had said I would.* Grabbing the sack, she hoisted it to her shoulder, pleased with how her strength had been slowly growing. Inside, the bag landed on the counter with a thud, "Here you go. I hope it's enough."

"Oh, heavens, yes," the older woman smiled her praise. "More than enough. Le's grab a saucepan, an' I'll show you how t' make th' gravy."

Watching intently, Bailey felt pleased with the niche she had found. As the cook's assistant, she had gained insight into the infrastructure of the community, and learned that although they could survive on their own if they had to, they still brought in supplies from the outside world; *such as the flour, rice and sugar in the Tate's basement.* She could not have been more pleased with the new knowledge the post had given her, as it helped her to feel that she did, in fact, belong.

She had learned after her arrival that meals were prepared in rotation, so that only half of them were served by the individual households. Breakfast every morning being the majority, they also consumed two or three dinners a week in homes. Other than that, everyone picked up plates at the designated location for lunches, and ate at the diner for the four or five evening meals, and they would be arriving shortly to enjoy this one.

Caleb had explained having only a few cooks allowed everyone else to focus on other chores. *That makes this a very important task,* she contemplated while she stirred the thickening mixture. She liked the feeling contributing and being useful gave her, and wore a small smile while her arm circled above the pot.

"Tha's perfect," Lynette peeked over at Bailey's handiwork. "I can't wait t' try it."

"Thanks," her green eyes shone when she cut them over at the shorter girl, "I learned from the best." Lyn giggled at her flattery, and began preparing the dishes for the serving line.

Bailey had been there for four weeks, and it felt good to be slowly gaining a bit of trust, at least with a portion of the group's members. It had almost felt like a promotion when she was given the job of using their electric cart to help with the process, mainly because it meant she had been allowed to know more about the secrets of their community.

And I found out the Knight stores are poisoned. She shuddered at the thought, realizing the gravity of the knowledge. She wondered why they would intentionally taint their own food, but not enough to push the issue and ask; *knowing not to eat it or serve it is enough, I guess.*

The discovery had left her feeling guilty after her

confrontation with her uncle and Jim, and the distress her cavalier attitude had caused them. She almost wanted to apologize to them, and she hoped the love and care she put into preparing their meals said what was in her heart clearly enough.

Watching the community members file in, Bailey located her brothers and made sure they were getting settled. "How was your day?" she asked cheerily, putting mashed potatoes on each of their plates.

"It was fun," Jess informed her, "We got to help with the stock tank over in the pasture today.

"Stock tank!" her eyes widened in surprise, "You guys have cattle?" she stared at Caleb as he moved into the line.

"We have a few. They are proving to be a bit more difficult than some o' the other animals," he admitted quietly. "So we'll see if they end up remaining one of our food sources, or if we butcher 'em an' be done with it. We also picked up a few goats, an' I think we'll have better luck with them."

"Nice," she grinned at the blond, and he remained behind for several minutes to chat with her. "Will I get my lesson this evening?" she eventually asked with a half grin.

"Sorry, little bit, got some business t' discuss this evenin'. I'll miss it though, an' maybe we can get together tomorrow," he winked with his reply and turned to walk away, taking his seat with a few of the men.

Bailey frowned, seeing that Amanda was also at the table with the group, and a twinge of jealousy twisted her gut for a moment.

Noticing Lynette had been listening to their exchange, Bailey's face flushed. Gathering a few of the empty serving bowls, she left the line to return them to the kitchen to be restocked. Placing the dishes on the flat surface a few minutes later, she made her own plate, and chose a table on the patio, away from the others so she could eat in peace and reflect upon her day.

Arriving at the ranch house after the diner and its kitchen were spotless, Bailey had her shower, knowing she needed to get to bed. The boys were already asleep, as life on The Ranch started early, and there were no excuses for letting the rest of the community down.

The following morning, Connie headed the girl off before she could make her way over to the greenhouse, and the field beyond. "You need t' hang aroun' here today. I got a few chores I need yur help with."

"Yes, ma'am," the girl gave no argument, taking the plates and starting on the dishes.

Growing up, Bailey had been taught that such tasks were beneath her, and delegated to the maid. However, being a part of The Ranch had caused her to see things differently. Every job had a purpose, and no ranking system could be ascertained. Each of them was valued as necessary, and she found that even being the maid was a place of honor. It was something she could aspire to, and she therefore no longer took offense at any job that they assigned to her.

She had worked her way in closer with the few who were willing to teach her, with the garden and with cooking the meals. So far, Connie had been a small part of her training, showing her the process of canning some of the vegetables and meats, and how to make preserves from the fruit of the various trees. Finishing with the cleanup, the girl hoped that today would hold more lessons along those lines, as she surely needed the practice.

Once all of the plates, glasses and flatware had been put away, the older woman began to give instructions, and the girl recalled that the group's matriarch had not officially made the nice list. *She tolerates me, but her actions cannot be construed as friendly.* Pleased to discover they would in fact be processing food, the pair dug into bushels of carrots and okra, canning the one, and pickling the other.

Completing that day's food storage during the morning, the older woman gave the girl an additional list of chores after lunch, "You need t' clean all three o' the bathrooms, an' don' forget to scrub out the showers. After that, strip down th' beds an' wash the sheets."

Bailey nodded, "Yes, ma'am. I can start the wash and scrub in between, if it would be faster."

"That'll be fine," the wrinkled hands began to take care of the kitchen for the second time that day.

Leaving her, the younger woman hurried up the stairs, stripping down all of the beds. While she worked, she considered what the men folk, as her brother put it, might be up to. She had only explored a small part of the compound, and had no idea what took place in several of the structures.

Heaving a deep sigh, she took the bunk bed sheets and uncle's items down first, placing them in the washer in the small room off the back of the kitchen. Connie watched her as she passed and caught her on the way out, "Be sure t' hang those out on th' line an' save the dryer."

Bailey adjusted the bucket of cleaning supplies in her grasp, giving the older woman a nod, "Yes, I will be sure." Making a quick exit, she went on to get started on the lavatories.

Working steadily, the girl made good time, washing the older couple's sheets along with the sets out of Devon and Nung's room. Tackling the second floor bathroom, she found it to be a little rougher than the first, but manageable. Making her way down the stairs with the final load of sheets, she noted that the matriarch of the community had been inspecting her work.

"Does it pass?" she gave the older woman a hint of a smile, not really intending to be sassy.

"It'll do," the crystal blue eyes shone at her, "I guess you're in charge o' them from now on."

Bailey nodded, somewhat relieved to finally have a job that would be designated as hers permanently. While they were talking, her brother came in, covered in the smelliest mud she had ever encountered. "What on earth have you been doing!" she exclaimed.

"Helping muck out the pig pens," he beamed. "I'm 'posed to get a bath."

"Not in my freshly cleaned tub, you're not! Come back outside and let's hose you off first." Leading him to the side yard, she stripped her younger sibling down to his cotton briefs and proceeded to use the garden sprayer to remove the majority of the filthy soil.

Giggling loudly, Jase seemed to be enjoying the attention when Jess joined them, equally as coated. "Is that what you guys do all day? And here I thought you were having fun," she teased.

"It is fun," Jess cackled, "We love working on the farm."

The girl only shook her head, content to allow them to think so, fairly certain the opinion would change after the novelty wore off. Once they were ready, she escorted them inside for a proper bath, and laid out clothes so they could dress for dinner. Giving the soiled items another rinse before taking them inside, she tossed them in the wash, carrying the last of the sheets out to the line.

While she finished the chores, her uncle came in to get ready for dinner as well, stopping long enough to watch while Bailey dealt with the boys. He had no kids of his own, and had thought he was really too old for it when they first got the call. *But this hasn't been half bad.*

He knew if he were honest about it, he and Brenda had been relieved they had never been blessed; *the world is doomed and it's better we didn't have any offspring to face the harsh times that lay ahead.*

Moving to the third floor, he washed his tired frame, and put on a clean set of clothes while mentally praising his niece's efforts. *She's got a good heart, and a strong work ethic; I only hope it'll be enough in the end.* Gathering his ready-made family, his face beamed with joy while they joked with one another as they joined the rest of the community for the evening meal at the diner.

Waiting in line, the crowd served their plates and enjoyed their dinner. Bailey again sat alone, watching her family and reflecting on her recent discoveries. Far away in thought, she didn't notice the tall blond until he slid onto the chair beside her, "Hey, little bit."

"Hey," a small grin spread across her features. "Do I get that lesson tonight?"

"Sure, if you're not too tired. I hear you've been workin' your ass off around here," he returned the smile.

"Well," she shrugged, "I've been busy; I'll say that. This's a hard life," she cut her eyes over at him. "Why anyone would choose to live like this is beyond me."

She could see him sucking in a deep breath, so she raised her hand to cut him off, "I'm joking, Caleb. My uncle has informed me of the crazy notions that seem to be the norm around here. I'm just attempting a little humor about this whole... situation," she wafted her hand at her neighbors.

"Yeah," he shrugged. "I guess I get it. I've been here all my life, so these notions aren't so crazy to me. Ya know?"

His smile gave Bailey a strange twist in her gut, and she flicked her eyes around, looking for the other tall blonde on the premises; "Yes, I know." Not locating the girl, she figured she was safe to enjoy the rest of her meal; *and the company.* Standing a few minutes later, they trained under their tree behind the stables until the sun had set and it was too dark to see.

Walking the girl home, Caleb noted she hadn't bothered putting on her makeup since her first day there. "You know, you look a lot better without all that stuff on your face."

Bailey cut her eyes over at him, surprised by the compliment. "Pretty pointless around here; it gets sweated off before lunch," she grinned. Arriving at the ranch house, she stepped onto the bottom step, and turned to face him, able to look him in the eye.

"I wanted to thank you, Caleb. You've turned out to be a really good friend." She stared into his smoky grey orbs, her mind briefly considering what he might taste like if she dared to kiss him, before reminding herself, *don't be silly.*

"Don' mention it," he smiled, lingering for a moment before taking an exaggerated step back. "Guess I'll see you in the morning. It's 'Manda's turn to lead, so there's no tellin' what she'll have cooked up for us."

"Oh, God," Bailey rolled her eyes, certain the girl would be out to get her, "Ok, I'll get some sleep and drag myself down there. I can't wait," she chuckled. Turning, she climbed the rest of the steps and made her way up to her room to do precisely that.

NO ONE ELSE

The following afternoon, Bailey entered the stables to find Caleb wasn't there. Turning to leave, she could hear noises at the far end of the structure, and made her way down to investigate. Inching her way closer, she made out the distinct sound of a woman whining or moaning. Hearing a man grunt loudly a few times, she froze, her face growing flushed at the realization of what was taking place in the last stall.

Unable to move, her mind ran in circles as she listened to the noisy couple, images of them leaping into her vivid imagination. A moment later, the thought occurred to her that Caleb and Amanda might have decided to kiss and make up. *Well, more than kiss,* she snapped her gaping mouth closed in disgust.

At that moment, a hand clamped onto her shoulder and she spun around with a gasp to find the man in question standing behind her. A single index finger pressed to his lips, he indicated for her to remain silent, and beckoned her to follow.

Nodding her agreement, Bailey felt obliged to do so, not daring to speak until they were beneath their usual tree, and only then in a low whisper. "Were they doing what it sounded like?" she demanded almost angrily.

"Yeah," he shrugged, somewhat embarrassed by her discovery, "That's generally the accepted place for *horsing around*, so don't go down there, little bit. Unless o' course you're looking t' get laid," he cut his eyes over at her, giving her a crooked grin.

Bailey clicked her tongue loudly, taken aback that he would speak to her that way.

Seeing her shocked expression, he back-pedaled quickly, "Sorry, that was a little uncalled for," and his face took on a slightly deeper shade of red.

Looking away, the girl glanced at the backside of the structure, aware that the couple was more than likely still going at it on the other side of the wall. "Who's in there, do you think?" she asked quietly, knowing that there were a large number of female possibilities, but the man could only be one of a few.

"Who knows," he lied flatly, well aware that Luis had been banging Judy for months, and he suspected that Don and Jennifer were also involved.

Shifting her eyes over at her closest friend, Bailey exhaled loudly, "This place is really messed up, you know that?"

Caleb only nodded, then raked the underside of her chin with a few fingers, "Yeah, I know that. Le's get started and forget about those guys," he indicated the lovers with a toss of his head.

Working through the day's lesson, Bailey tried to remain focused. Her mind kept drifting away, still trapped inside the wooden walls, and her first realization that more went on in the shadows of the small community than she had realized.

It bothered her deeply that they would carry on in that manner; having casual sexual relationships had never been her thing. Furthermore, she failed to see how this group would stand for it. *After all, they're worried about an outsider, when their flippant attitudes could just as easily destroy everything as well.*

When they had finished and stretched out on the ground, she pushed the issue, "Ok really, who was inside the barn?"

"I'm not gonna tell you that, little bit," he calmly plucked a blade of grass to chew on.

"Well, at least tell me why they're hiding to do it. Isn't anything sacred around here?" her nose wrinkled in disgust.

Caleb glared at her from his reclined position, recalling the night he had pulled her out of the bushes after beating the shit out of the guy who had put her there. "Are you really a virgin?" he demanded.

Locking her jaw, she avoided looking at him. *Son of*

a bitch. "So what if I am? You know, not all cheerleaders are sluts." She exhaled loudly, "I just want the first time to be… perfect." She paused for a long moment, "I want it to be the right guy. The one I will spend my life with, and no one else." Her voice had grown quiet as she finished.

Chewing on a fresh piece, the young man pointed it at her for a moment, "You know, most people don' believe in that these days."

"Yes," she sighed her agreement, "I know. I see it all around us. But I thought here might be different; I guess not." Standing abruptly, she walked away, having learned more that day than she would have liked to.

Caleb watched her long shadow disappear around the corner, headed for the ranch house he presumed. Continuing to lay sprawled beneath the tree, his mind wandered back to his break-up with Amanda, and he recalled that sex had been the end of their relationship.

"Why can't we?" the tall blonde had cooed, running her hands up his chest and caressing his neck while she inched him towards the last stall of the barn. "We're old enough," she pleaded in her soft, sultry voice, "An' I'm tired o' waitin'."

Catching her digits, Caleb had peered into her pale blue eyes, "You know what your ol' man'll do if he finds out I'm fuckin' you? Besides, we're gonna get married, aren't we? So what's wrong with waitin' until then?"

The girl had pulled her fingers free, continuing to try

and persuade him, to no avail. Eventually, he had dragged himself away, leaving her in the stables and taking a long walk; alone.

Little did he know, another man had been standing in the shadows, watching the couple. Coming out of his hiding place, under the guise of consoling the distraught young woman, someone else had claimed her that night, as she had been easy to convince in her excited state.

The memory of their fight a few days later crushed in around him. *Fucking slut*, Caleb cursed his former girlfriend again as he stretched and stood. Deep down, he had berated himself at the time, thinking it had been his fault in a way, having not given in to her desires. She had fed his feelings of regret, claiming she was sorry she had wasted her first time with someone else.

Today, he knew better; the girl had made the rounds, having been with all four of the unattached males that lived in the ranch house. *Hell, she may've even given ol' Pete a toss or two.* She wasn't sorry, and didn't mind rubbing it in his face that she was far more worldly than himself.

With a heavy sigh, he shook his head as he made his way over to finish up with the caged animals before he called it a night. *Yes sir, little bit, if you're really savin' it for Mr. Right, that makes you pretty rare in these parts indeed.* Putting his thoughts back onto his chores, he tried not to think any more about the fiery highlights that seemed to be setting his heart ablaze.

APPEARANCES

Bailey blinked into the darkness, and lay quietly listening to the creaking of the windmill for several minutes. Her mind turning, she thought about how she had awoken in that same bed every day for a month. It seemed much longer, and so much about her had changed.

She hated to think of herself as self-absorbed, but she could admit the truth, at least to herself. These days she felt more aware of the people around her, as if the small group of strangers had slowly worked its way inside her, in a way no one before ever had.

Some of them she still did not feel comfortable with. And some she felt sorry for. Most of the young people there had hardly ever been outside the gates of the small fortress, and learning that had given her a better perspective into their thoughts and understanding of the world.

Eventually tossing back her covers, she put on the clothes she wore to work out, and quietly made her way down stairs. Running as fast as she could, she pushed herself to make a lap around the outside wall, arriving in front of the gym to begin whatever torture the day's leader had in store for them.

The group seemed small that morning, but she gave each a smile and a friendly hello, noting that Caleb was not among them. Once they had gone over the routine, and begun the workout, she found her eyes being drawn to the four men who shared her floor in the stately structure she currently called home.

Aware that they sometimes watched her, her mind drifted back to her discoveries the previous afternoon. *I wonder which one it had been.* She couldn't stop the image and question from invading her thoughts. *It had to be one of them; otherwise it was a married man.* Her breath caught in her lungs at the top of a sit-up, *oh my God! Surely it wasn't Peter.*

The idea that her uncle could do such a thing, especially since all of the girls were at least thirty years younger than him, made her want to vomit. *No,* she told herself firmly; *it wasn't him.* Standing, she strutted over to the bars and began to do a round of pull-ups. While she hung there, she noticed Caleb coming in late, and breathed a small sigh of relief.

The man brought mixed emotions into her scattered being, and she found comfort in simply knowing where he was and what he was doing. *Didn't I warn you once to stay away from him?* she teased herself, while hoisting her body up and her chin to the rail.

A few minutes later, she dropped down to the floor, ready to do her push-ups and begin the next round. "You're late," she taunted when he landed beside her.

"Yeah, had to have a talk with my ol' man," he supplied quietly.

"Oh? Anything I need to know about?" she grinned, aware that there would probably be nothing that would even qualify.

Shooting her a quick smirk, he winked, "Not this time, little bit." Jumping up, he headed for the bars.

Half an hour later, their workout had been completed. A few of them occupied the showers there, while everyone else returned to their homes to bathe, dress and move on with their day. Once Bailey had done the same, she made her way down the stairs to join the others for breakfast.

Seeing that the rest had started without her, she fixed her plate of eggs, bacon and toast. Her brothers were unusually quiet, so she cleared her throat loudly, preparing to find out why. "Hey fellas, what's up?" she inquired casually, trying to cover her concern.

Jess, seated closest to her, looked at her with doleful eyes, and spoke with a trembling lip, "We miss mom and dad."

Her jaw dropped slightly at the utterance, and she wondered what had provoked the sudden realization of their absence. "Oh, honey," she looped her arm around him, dragging his smaller body against her. "Baby, I know you do."

Running her hand up and down his back, she could feel the small spasms that signaled his tears, and she could feel the eyes of the adults upon her while she held him. "It's ok, baby," she tried to comfort him, laying her cheek on the top of his straight brown hair. Gazing at the other twin who sat watching them, she noticed his eyes growing misty as well.

"I wish there was something I could do to make it better," she offered quietly, "But at least we've still got each other." She smiled at them, lifting her head and pushing him away enough she could look him in the eye. "You do like it here, don't you?"

"Yeah," he admitted quietly, "But it's not the same. I wanna go home."

Bailey could feel her heart being torn to shreds as she pulled him back to her, stroking his short dark strands. "I know, baby," she whispered, "And I know it's hard to understand," she tried to console him, her own emotions tangled on the subject. "But this is where we belong now."

Hearing her words, the boy yanked himself free, and looked at her with an angry pout, "No, we don't!" he tossed at her before he bolted from the room, Jase following quickly behind him.

Turning to sit correctly in her seat, the girl put her elbows on the table and folded her hands in front of her face, as if to pray. Not looking at any of the others, she could still feel them watching her, so she asked quietly, "Did something happen? Something to them, I don't know about?" She cut her eyes over at her uncle, waiting for someone to respond.

"No," he finally replied, "They're just goin' through the process, that's all. Grief takes time."

Bailey shifted the glare to the others, moving from left to right, finding their features to hold a variety of emotional states. In the end, none of them appeared angry, and the woman on the end actually looked quite sad. Her thoughts leapt to the aunt she couldn't remember; the one Caleb had described as a really nice lady.

"My aunt; Brenda. She was your daughter, wasn't she?" she spoke to the older woman quietly.

"Yeah," Connie agreed with a sniffle. "She was. An' I can sure tell you, there's no greater pain on earth than t' bury yur child. We still have two daughters livin' close at hand, but we'll always mourn the one we lost."

The room remained quiet for several minutes, and eventually everyone returned to their food, needing the nourishment for the day ahead. When she had finished, Bailey gathered plates and took them to the kitchen, helping to wash them before she made her way over to the garden.

"Be sure to pick a bushel o' beans today," Connie reminded her, "We need to stay ahead on the cannin', an' I know you like t' help."

"Yes, ma'am," the girl replied softly, giving the older woman a tiny smile. "I'll bring them when I come back for lunch." True to her word, the young woman gathered the requested bushel, and carried it with her when she entered through the back door some hours later.

Connie nodded at her young charge, pleased that she had become more than an outsider in the last few weeks. Putting the basket on the counter, the women made their way over to the Knight's dwelling, the day's lunch location, to fix their plates. Returning home a short time later, they set to work, spending the afternoon preparing and canning the fresh vegetables.

During the process, Connie saw fit to share a few stories of her daughters, and even granddaughters, all of whom lived at The Ranch with them. Her dark mood lightened in the telling, she gave away more of their secrets than any of the group had before, even revealing that everyone at the ranch was related to the Foxes somehow, by blood or by marriage. Everyone that is, except the Crosses, and the four loners who shared her floor, who came into the group purely on friendship.

Bailey could sense the close-knit feel of the community in the older woman's words, and briefly considered that it could be a reason for the girl from the stables to behave so secretively. *Perhaps they don't think their elders would approve; maybe that's why they hide.* The idea gave her new angles to consider, especially since she had grown up in a house where keeping up appearances had been of the utmost importance.

LAND OF THE FREE

Scattered across the grass in front of the airstrip, with the playground to their left, the small township eagerly waited for dark to settle completely over them, and for the show to begin. The Fourth of July, they would hold a small celebration for the land of the free, as they did every year. Bailey easily picked up on the happy vibes emanating off of almost everyone, and allowed herself to fall into the festive occasion.

Spreading a blanket on the grass, the boys eagerly flanked her and she held them in turn, hugging them and thanking God she had discovered how much she truly loved them. It had been three days since she had consoled them over breakfast, and since then, she had taken a more active role in their daily lives, making sure to check in on them and find out what they were up to.

When the first few lights burst above them, she listened to their gasps of joy, and a wide smile spread across her face. Glancing around at their new neighbors and friends, she had a strange feeling that many weren't watching the display; she felt as if they were observing them.

Bailey knew that the boys were the youngest people in the community, but with a wry grin she contemplated that it wouldn't be that way for long. *Not if some of the older girls are sleeping around.* She had a hunch it was only a matter of time before there would be more mouths to feed.

Tightening her grip on Jase, her thoughts drifted back to the previous afternoon and a conversation she had had with John Cross. He had met her at the stables, instead of Caleb. It had shocked her to the point of panic when he used a casual tone to inquire about their relationship as soon as she had entered the dark chamber.

"I hear you've enlisted my son t' train you," he had said, stroking the horse in front of him, "That you've decided t' learn to fight. Any particular reason why?"

Bailey had never spoken to the man before, and his deep round tone frightened her to a degree. "I thought it might be smart," she replied timidly, sidling up closer and observing his hands as they moved. "Caleb's a good teacher."

"You don' feel safe here?" he had demanded a little more firmly.

"Feel safe?" she echoed, unsure if she should voice her true concerns. "I guess that I do." She looked around at the stalls, listening to the noises of the animals for a moment. "I didn't ask him because I was afraid," she confessed, "I did it because I was angry."

"Angry?" he scoffed lightly, "'Bout what?"

"About Amanda," she spoke quietly, shifting her gaze to the ground between them. "She beat me up."

"An' that pissed you off, did it," John replied with a laugh, "Thinkin' you might get even at some point."

"Something like that," the girl shrugged. "Caleb says that you made sure everyone who lives here was trained; how to fight, how to shoot, lots of things." She raised her chin as if to challenge the older man. "They say you guys are getting ready for the end of the world."

He stopped short, turning to look at her squarely, "But that don' scare you?"

"No," she chirped crisply, "I don't think it does. My life here is very different than it had been, before my parents died. When we first got here, I think that I was afraid; but mostly I was sad because of everything that I had lost."

"Caleb says you're strong," John countered, "Says you would be a good addition to our community. Everyone else," he paused, returning to his work, "Well, they're not s' sure."

"Take care of my brothers then, ok?"

"What's that supposed t' mean?" he cut his glare back over to her.

"It means, if you decide to get rid of me, or send me

away, or whatever. I mean, you guys are obviously happy to have them here, the way you all fawn over them. Maybe because you're short on boys, I don't know," she kept her eyes on him, watching for his reaction to her hypothesis.

"I guess you noticed our ratio is a little off," he chuckled.

"Yes," she sighed loudly, "I noticed. That's why I figure you'll send me away. You don't really have room for another girl. So when you do, please just take care of them. Ok?"

She had turned to go, ready to end the uncomfortable conversation, when he called to her in a low voice, "There's always room here for you, Bailey. But only if this is th' place you choose t' be." She had walked away, skipping their lesson for the day, and using the time to ponder what her friend's father had said, and what he might have meant.

Leaning against her brother on the blanket, she reached up and stroked his brown hair. They had been training them as well, at least it appeared so from what she had learned in the last few days. It had made her angry, back when her uncle had first taught them to play violent video games, but she had realized later that they were desensitizing them; preparing them to accept certain things without question.

She had found her way into the gun range, where Carson gave them lessons for shooting his twenty-two, and she had to admit, they appeared to be really good at it. Her family had never believed in guns, so she had never touched one. *After I finish the hand to hand stuff, maybe I could try some of the weapons for myself; if they* would allow it, of course.

Staring up into the sky, she allowed her mind to relax, happy to be living in that moment with her younger siblings; content to be celebrating with the group of people who had reluctantly taken them in.

Unexpectedly, a male body dropped down on the blanket next to her, "Hey guys. How you like the show?"

"It's great!" Jess beamed, the varied colors lighting up his face while he scooted into the man's lap.

Bailey smiled, relieved to see that the boys were again enjoying their lives on The Ranch. She still wanted to take them away from there, when the time was right, but for now it was nice to see them happy, and growing strong.

Leaning slightly towards the older male, she whispered loudly, "You know. I think people are going to notice us spending so much time together." She cut her eyes over at him, aware that he did not meet her gaze.

"Yeah," he nodded slightly, "They noticed. Had a talk with my ol' man about you."

"I know. He and I had a heart to heart yesterday; that's why I skipped our lesson." She paused, curious about his take on their relationship, and the odd vibes she still picked up from him on occasion, "You told him we're just friends, right?"

"Hmmph," Caleb grimaced, "Yeah, he knows. He likes you, I think. Not sure how mom feels, though."

"Really? I don't think anyone around here likes me. Mostly, they tolerate me. But it's getting better, I guess, and I'm not as scared as I was," she admitted quietly, aware of the boys seated on the cloth with them.

"You were scared?" the blond finally cast her a quick glance.

"Of course I was," she giggled nervously, "A strange place, with crazy ideas floating around. I think I would have been foolish not to have been afraid."

"You're gonna be fine, little bit," he gave her a full smile. "No one's gonna hurt you. In fact, there's talk of taking you back to Midland for your final year."

Bailey could feel the lump in her throat, her heart pounding wildly inside her chest, "Oh my God, really?"

"Yeah," he nodded, "So hang in there."

"Ok," she glanced around, still feeling like more people were watching them than the display, "When?"

"I dunno. Nothing's official yet. In time for school to start, maybe a few weeks before. We can talk about the rest later," he stroked the smaller head in his lap while he spoke.

"Sure," she smiled in earnest, curious if her brothers would be included in the proposition. *But at least I'm going to get another chance,* she breathed. *There for the longest time, I thought this would be the last home I would ever know.*

TELL ME EVERYTHING

After the Fourth of July celebration, Bailey began to relax into life on The Ranch. Her fear of being harmed by the other community members had waned after her confrontation with John Cross, and she firmly believed that if they intended to kill her, they would have done so already. Her conversation with Caleb had confirmed this, and she could at last look forward to the future with hope.

Still driven by the desire to even the score with Amanda, she refrained from attempting to make friends with the girl. Everyone else on the premises, however, became fair game, and she slowly made the rounds, getting closer to as many as she could, while trying to learn about them and their past.

One of the first few that she became better acquainted with was Alissa Porter. She had the honor of being the youngest of the Fox daughters, and explained that she had married her husband Tom in an attempt to avoid coming to The Ranch, back when her parents first made the move.

"I got pregnant with Judy on purpose, so I guess you could say I trapped him," she confessed while they picked tomatoes in the morning sun. "I was only sixteen at the time. He loved me though, an' we had Lynnette a few years later."

Bailey grimaced, "So how did you end up here?"

"He died," her expression shifted to sad for a moment, "He worked on an oil rig an' they had some kinda accident. When th' case settled, I decided to bring the money and invest it here, in th' community."

The girl bobbed her head lightly, having wondered how they had managed to fund such a massive enterprise, "You got enough to pay for all this?" she wafted her hand around to indicate the expanse of the fortress.

"Oh, hell no," Alissa laughed, "Only a small part. The thing is, everyone contributes. Some o' the men take jobs an' work outside to bring in income. An' we never keep cash; we always invest it somewhere. Cash won' be worth anything when the end comes." Her features grew strained after she let the last sentence slip.

"It's ok," Bailey soothed, "I know the reason behind building The Ranch."

"Oh, you do?" she breathed in relief, "I'm so glad! I thought I had told you somethin' I shouldn't have!"

"No, you're good. So, how long have you actually

been here?" she pushed for more, realizing that the Porter girls had spent some time on the outside if what she said was true.

"Tom's been gone eight years. We moved here right after Lynnette's tenth birthday, so about six years," she replied, topping off her basket, "I think we've plucked enough for today. Le's get these over t' Martha's so she can get started on them."

"Is she going to can them?" Bailey asked, with the mason jars they always used coming to mind.

"Yes, we can most everything," the other woman explained, "Makes it last longer. Plus we keep a rotation going, so we're eatin' the stuff that was stored in previous years, an' save the fresher crops for the future."

"Yes, I noticed you guys had a pretty good way of keeping track," Bailey beamed at the discovery, "Pretty smart."

"You think it'll work? If we ever truly need it?"

"I don't know why it wouldn't," she nodded her approval, "What I don't get is what could be so catastrophic that the world would actually come to an end." She resisted the urge to make fun of their concern over the volcano a few weeks back.

Alissa laughed, "Well, that depends on who you talk to. Some here think that there's gonna be a huge pandemic, an' some crazy illness will circle the globe, killin' off everyone. So bein' away, in the middle o' nowhere means we got that covered."

"Right," Bailey agreed. "What do you believe will be the cause? Are you a zombie apocalypse kinda girl?" she giggled at her joke.

"Uhh, no," she replied, placing her basket on the Cross porch, "I think that in the end, it'll be men killin' each other that'll bring about our demise. Maybe a nuclear war. Maybe some chemical bombings or somethin'. Somethin' really gruesome like that, which means again, keepin' away will help us have a better chance."

"You guys sound like you've thought of everything," Bailey praised.

"Well, we've tried to. Le's go find lunch shall we?" Alissa ended the conversation at that, hoping that she really hadn't revealed too much, and knowing that things wouldn't go well for her if she had.

After their meal, the girls went their separate ways, and Bailey wandered over to the stables. Finding a shady spot in the back, she stretched out, considering a nap before her combat lesson; *if he has time for me today.*

"Hey, stranger," Caleb teased, towering over her reclined position beneath their tree.

"Hey yourself," Bailey countered, grinning from ear to ear, *there goes my nap.* "I have a question for you, once we get started."

"Alright, le's go!" he offered her his hand and hauled her to her feet.

Once they were into the routine, she put forth her quandary, "How do you think the world is going to end? Tell me everything, and don't worry about upsetting me."

"Why the hell are you asking me that?" he stopped in mid-movement and glared at her.

"I don't know, just curious I guess. I mean, you guys have gone to a lot of trouble to build this place, and I'm trying to figure out if it was really worth it." She could see his eyes grow distant, and second guessed herself, "It's ok if you don't want to talk about it," she added quickly.

"Naw, I'll tell you what I think. Only, I don' understand why you wanna know," he blinked at her, his mind turning what her motives could be. "Le's finish this up, an' then we'll take a walk."

She noticed that he looked around them, appearing to be anxious while they went through the rest of his lesson, and she did her best to focus the remainder of the time. Once they were done, they took off to stroll around the base of the massive wall.

"You seem nervous," she prodded gently, "Does it bother you to think about it?"

"A little bit," he confessed. "I guess because I never really believed it would happen. Not when I was a kid, anyways."

"And you grew up here," she recalled.

"Yeah, I've never lived anywhere else. I mean, I've

stayed other places, mostly in Midland or Odessa. I spent some time in El Paso, too, when I was workin' or whatever," he kicked the ground anxiously, "But this has always been my home."

"So, what made you change your mind," she squinted slightly at him, "That the end is really going to come."

"The world's just got so many things wrong with it," he used his hands to illustrate, "And at the very base of all of it is man. We're destroyin' our planet, an' each other. I only hope when it reaches critical, there's still enough o' nature left for the earth to heal itself an' t' go on."

"What's your favorite theory then? How's mankind going to meet its doom?"

"I like another ice age. That'll wipe out a few billion pretty efficiently," he chuckled slightly, "O' course that's not really how I see it goin' down. I think over all, the greatest thing we have goin' against us is each other. Our planet is grossly overpopulated, an' we're shipping resources all over the place, instead o' livin' off o' what's available locally. That's one o' the reason's I like this set up here."

"Ok, anything specific?"

"Well, we could live indefinitely off o' what we're able t' produce here. With the wind power for electricity an' water, we could go without anything from the outside world. An' with the multiple systems, we have backups, so if we did encounter a problem, we would have time to make an alternate plan or repair it."

"So you think shipping food to other areas is a no-no?"

"Oh hell yeah! Take Midland for example. It's in the middle o' the desert, for Christ's sake!"

Bailey grinned at his assessment, having discovered the same thing for herself a few months prior. "Ok, so why is that important? I mean, technically, so is The Ranch."

He laughed at her naivety, "Yeah, but we're not trying to support a million people here. If anything, or when anything, ever happens, all those people are fucked," he held his hands up, palms to the sky, "There's no resources aroun' there, so as soon as things even get a little bumpy, it has the potential t' get ugly."

"You think they would hurt each other?" she scowled heavily.

"Most definitely," he shoved his hands in his pockets, kicking the ground again. "Once the food runs out, an' the stores are emptied, the smart ones are gonna get the hell out o' town an' the rest'll be fightin' over the scraps."

"Wow," she breathed, "That's a scary thought."

Caleb stopped abruptly, "I know it is, little bit. That's why I really hope you decide to stay here."

"You really think that I'm going to get a choice? Uncle Pete said when we came here we would go back to the apartment so I could finish high school, but then afterwards he said I couldn't leave. I wish he would make up his mind."

"Well, I think he already has," he spun on his heel, looking around them to see if anyone were close by, "I wasn't supposed to tell you. But, you're gonna find out soon enough anyways. They're sendin' you back to Midland, alright, in a few days. I think the boys're stayin' here though."

"What?" she cried a little loudly, disappointed she had been right about them being forced to remain behind.

"Sshssh," he waved his hands at her anxiously, "I jus' said I wadn'supposed t' tell you, so you can't say anything. But yeah, I'm pretty sure that's what's gonna happen. They're gonna keep th' boys though, so they aren't uprooted again when you come back."

"And if I don't come back, then they're just rid of me, is that it?" she fumed.

"Something like that," he confessed, reaching for her hand. "It's a big choice, little bit."

"Well, that's just great. Am I going alone, or is Uncle Pete coming?"

"I don't know the particulars," he sighed, dropping her digits and ambling along the path. "An' Pete's a petroleum engineer; he mostly works in the field or as a consultant. He only took the office job there in town for those few months so you guys could finish out the school year. But, he may go and stay with you sporadically, t' give you a little supervision."

"Are you coming?" she asked more quietly. "I mean, I'm sure there are people here who could take care of the horses." The evening sun glinted off his blond spikes, and she could see how he worked to process the question.

"I'm not sure if I should do that," he replied softly, leaving the reasons for his doubts unspoken. He would have liked to tell her that he didn't want to go, because it might influence her decision, but the last thing he wanted was to taint her choice. In the end, he knew he couldn't do that, so the best option would be to allow her to do it all on her own.

RENDERED

Bailey climbed the stairs to her room that night with a heavy heart. She hadn't wanted to come to The Ranch to begin with, but the thought of leaving made her weary with grief. *Maybe you don't want to leave the twins; maybe that's it.* She tried to console herself, knowing they were in good hands, but in the end, she knew that wasn't the cause of her anguish.

Stripping down and slipping into her light pajamas, she climbed under her quilt and stared at the window, aware of the windmill outside. *I'm going to miss this place,* she confessed into the darkness. *And I'm going to miss Caleb.*

Never in her life had the girl worked so hard. Her hands had grown tougher, after the hours of working in the garden. And she had quickly gotten used to the idea of going without makeup, trading the time she used to spend working on her appearance for the hours she put into building her health and strength.

I wonder what they would think, if I refused to go. She toyed with the idea, aware that it wouldn't be a wise choice. She knew she needed to complete her education, and that going to the high school for one more year was the best option.

She also knew that Jess and Jase would be home schooled, along with the rest of the kids at The Ranch, so she didn't have to worry about that. The rest of the young people there seemed pretty well off, so she felt confident that it would be comparable to public education; *Caleb is taking college classes after all.*

Still, she had much to consider, with all of their lives being affected by her choice. Knowing she had a few days to decide, she put the decision on the back burner, and focused on her breathing until she fell asleep.

Time passed and things continued as normal, Bailey feeling aware that the friendships she had started to build continued to grow. She found herself lost each day in the never ending list of chores and lessons that occupied her time. In the end, no one mentioned her leaving for a full month, and she had begun to wonder if Caleb had been wrong by the time her uncle approached her.

"Hey, Bailey-girl," Pete sidled up next to her while she enjoyed a sunset on the veranda with the boys. "Are you about ready t' get back t' civilization?"

Her mouth gaping, she stared at him, having thought the day would never come. "I guess that I am," she breathed in deep pants of excitement, "Is it time to go back to school?" She hadn't been sure what her choice would be, until it had been laid before her. *I need to go and finish, that's all there is to it.*

"Yeah," he looked away from her, taking in the gorgeous sky, "The boys are gonna join the small school here locally, but I think it would be better if we let you finish the last year in Midland; if you wanna go."

"Yes, I'll go," she beamed, "But you guys will be here when I get back right? I've gotten kind of attached to these guys," she tussled a set of brown locks for emphasis.

Grinning, Pete stepped forward, pulling her into a tight embrace. "Be good, little bit," he urged into her hair, "Get your things together tonight; Luis's gonna take the plane an' fly you back first thing in the morning."

"What do you mean, Luis?" she stammered, "You're not taking me?"

"Naw," he countered smoothly, "I got things to do around here. The guys'll give you a lift, an' he's gonna stay at the apartment with you; get a job an' all that. Just take your key and do your best. You're old enough, and responsible enough," he sighed loudly. "Make good choices, an' we'll see you maybe for Christmas."

"Yes, sir," she grinned broadly, giving him a mock salute. Grabbing each of her little brothers for a quick hug, she headed up the stairs to pack her bag and be ready to leave. *So, Luis is going to be my chaperone. I wonder who else is going to bring the plane back?*

While stuffing her things into her suitcase, she realized she wouldn't need much. Mostly her makeup, as she had left the rest of her belongings at the apartment. Running down a mental check list, she made sure her key and her phones were in the side of her bag and she was set.

At that moment, her thoughts turned to the fair haired man who had become her trainer and dearest friend. *I have to see Caleb.* She knew it would be hard, but she couldn't bear the thought of leaving without saying goodbye.

Clomping down the stairs, she noticed how late it was getting, and most of the house had turned in for the night. *Gosh, I'll have to hurry if I want to be discrete.* She could always knock on his door, but the thought of disturbing his parents tarnished the idea.

Hoping he would still be out with the animals, she jogged down the road that connected the ranch house to the barn and stables. Opening the door quietly, she listened into the darkness, the stillness indicating that the far stall remained unoccupied that evening.

Back outside, she made her way over to the barn, to the end with the swinging double doors, which held the cages of rabbits. She gave a startled jump when the door opened and the man she had been searching for stepped out into the moonlight.

"Hey, little bit, what a surprise," he grinned, but his brow appeared furrowed in dim glow. "You all set t' leave?"

"Yes," she breathed quietly, falling into step beside him, "But I realized I needed to see you before I left." Her face flushed, and she felt happy for the darkness that would cover for her, "You want to go sit beneath the tree for a few minutes?"

He stared at her for a moment, his heart heavy. *Damn. This is so hard.* "Sure," he replied softly, surprising her by catching her fingers as they moved. "You know, I'm really gonna miss you," he supplied when they arrived at the twisted branches.

"I'm going to miss you, too," she smiled up at him, wondering if a goodbye kiss would be in order, before she tossed the idea.

Caleb stared down at her blankly, his mind racing. *She really doesn't know.* Gasping for air, he thought he might cry. *So trusting. What the hell are you gonna do about it though?* "Hey," he grinned genuinely, "You know, I never did take you for that ride."

Laughing loudly, she agreed, "I know; too busy I guess. We'll have to save it for when I get back."

"Le's do it now," he offered, overcome with the idea.

Bailey chuckled again, "Now? It's late; won't everyone be going to bed?"

"It's ok," he shrugged, "I'll push it out th' front gate before we start it an' we can take a quick run; up the road an' back. Whadda ya say? No one gets disturbed that

way. Slip home an' grab a jacket, an' meet me there."
Not waiting for a reply, he took off, ready to retrieve his
ride from the garage behind his parents' house.

Staring after him when he left her, the girl shook her
head slowly; *crazy goof.* Part of her thought the idea
silly, but deep down she felt eager to join him on their
last adventure together before she made her way back to
the city.

Almost skipping down the path, she crept into the
ranch house, taking the stairs much more quietly this
time. Locating the sweatshirt and hoodie that she had
packed for cooler evenings, she carried them both with
her, and headed for the front gate. When she arrived,
Caleb had the motorcycle waiting outside, and hit the
keypad to close the large covering behind her.

"We won't be gone long, will we?" she asked,
growing a little nervous that it might upset someone that
they had.

"Not too long," he reassured.

Pulling both articles on, the girl adjusted the hood
portion over her ears and slid onto the back seat behind
him. Working her arms around, the engine seemed loud,
and she gripped him tightly, emitting a low squeal as the
pavement began to move beneath them.

The ride felt thrilling, her excitement only partially
caused by the rush of air against them. Digging her
fingers into his chest, she smiled at the thought of him,
and how much he had come to mean to her in the few

months she had known him. Resting her head against his back, she sighed her joy that she had chosen to take the ride with him.

She still wore a small elated grin when they reached the cattle guard at the end of their private road and pulled out onto the main highway to turn around. Stopping on the far side, Caleb killed the engine and swung off the bike, facing her. She thought he might have wanted to talk, but instead he slid his arms around her, placing his palm against the back of her head and holding her against him. Exhaling a loud breath, he dared to let his feelings show, if only for the moment.

"I can't do this," he whispered into her auburn locks, nuzzling her ear. Her uncle had filled him in on the parts of their plan she wouldn't find out about until it was too late, and he had been wrestling with the issue ever since. He knew he needed to take her someplace safe, and what's worse... he knew what it was going to cost him if he did.

Unsure what he couldn't do, Bailey looped her arms around him while still straddling his bike. Finding herself caught up in the rush of being close to him, she sighed, curious if he wanted to kiss her as well. The thrill of the idea gave her quivers of excitement, and she stroked the nape of his neck tenderly in anticipation.

To her surprise, he extracted himself from her grasp and slid back onto the seat in front of her. Restarting the engine, he allowed her to cling to him once more. Only, he didn't steer them back towards the compound.

Instead, he headed down the highway, rolling north. Deciding he wasn't ready to end the ride, she continued to hold on to him, growing weary as the hour grew late. A short time later, they pulled up at the small convenience store, surrounded by open pasture; the same one they had stopped at on the way down from Midland a few months before.

Although the interior appeared dark, the pumps beneath the awning were the twenty-four hour kind, with a credit card slot. Coming to a stop, Caleb killed the engine and opened the tank.

"I guess we'll head back now," she gave him a weak smile, standing herself to stretch her legs. The thrill of the moment had passed, and she only wanted to get some sleep.

Without looking at her, he inserted the nozzle, "I can't take you back."

Bailey could feel the air slowly escape from her chest, "What do you mean, you can't take me back? Why the hell not?" She sidled up next to him, reaching to grab his arm.

Twisting his appendage, he caught her hand and pulled her up so that his face lay right above hers, and he could glare into her perfect green orbs, "They weren't takin' you to Midland, little bit," he breathed. "If you had gotten on that plane..." his voice trailed away.

She could see his eyes squeezed into slits, the crystal

blue boring into her, "You said that everything was ok," her voice grew small.

"Yeah, I know," he nodded generously, turning back to the hose and closing the tank. "I thought that it was. But The Ranch's full o' people, an' in the end, it's a lot of responsibility, keepin' everyone safe."

"So I was too much of a threat?" she asked angrily.

"Something like that. If you got on the plane; if you chose t' leave... the guys were to take you away so the boys thought you had gone to school. Then, when you didn't come back next year, it would be because you had chosen not to." He cut his eyes over at her, waiting for her response.

Bailey glared at him, anger boiling, "And we left them there?!?" her voice grew shrill.

"Your brothers are fine. They were always wanted; needed. You're the one no one really cared about," his face dropped to plant his chin against his chest, ashamed of the part he had played in the group's sinister plot.

"So what do we do? Go back and get them?" she demanded bitterly.

"No," his gaze shot up to meet hers, "No, we go on to Midland. We can stay at the apartment. I'll get a job an' you can go t' school."

"Won't they just come after us, if they want to get rid of me that bad?"

"I don't think so," he heaved a deep breath, "I think

we'll be fine. Anyways, I'll contact my dad in a day or two, an' make peace." Reaching up, he caught a few auburn curls, tugging on them lightly. "I'm sorry. I really wanted everything to work out."

Glaring at him beneath the fluorescent glow of the canopy, her heart pounded wildly inside her chest. "This is insane," her mind screamed at her in warning. "I can't believe they would really hurt me," she whispered.

Caleb only grimaced, ready to put her back on the bike and be on their way. *Believe it, little bit,* he mentally challenged, *and you wouldn't be the first.*

Sneak Peek of RETAINED

Book 2 of the Irrevocable Series

Available July 14, 2015

PROLOGUE

Peter Mason ambled down the hall, waking the boys and preparing for their day. Glancing up the stairs, towards the third floor, his chest ached. But, in the end, he knew he couldn't let it show. Making his way to the bathroom, he slogged through his routine and worked his way to the kitchen, where a pot of coffee awaited.

Taking his place at the table, the boys joined him, smiling and digging into the morning meal before them. Watching the pair, he ate a few bites of the delicious scrambled eggs, not enjoying them nearly enough. Folding his hands under his chin, he put his elbows on the table, still stuck in his funk while he stared at the empty place at their side.

Pete had been trapped between the needs of his community and those of his niece for a while. In the end, his attempt had been small, almost feeble, and probably not enough to save her. Of course, what he had done was enough to disrupt all their lives if anyone were to find out. *Just breathe,* he reminded himself; *you'll know how it worked out before the day is over.*

"Hey, guys," he leapt to his feet, his heart skipping a beat when Luis and Devon came through the door. Not hesitating for a moment, the two disappeared through the other passage, and he followed them onto the front porch. "I thought you were taking care of Bailey this morning," his voice dropped in agitation.

"We gotta problem," the shorter man gasped with hands on his hips.

"What kinda problem," Pete shifted, already uneasy at their plans; having issues only made it worse.

"Da girl's gone," Devon supplied, leaning his tall frame against the railing, "All 'er stuff's still in 'er room, too."

"Yeah," Luis corroborated his story. "We scoured the entire compound, comin' up empty."

Peter stared at the pair, his jaw slightly hanging, and gasped, "You're kidding me. An' no one's seen her?"

"No one we talked to, no," Devon turned, hunching

over the top rail and scanning the horizon through narrowed slits.

"Did you talk to Bill? Surely, he doesn't think that I had anything to do with this!"

Luis shook his head slowly, "It wasn't you." Staring, he waited for the older man to make the connection.

"Caleb," Pete shook his honey and silver waves, "Son of a bitch!" He feigned surprise, careful to keep the grin from breaking through to the surface.

"So whadda we do?" Luis wrung his hands eagerly.

"We need a meeting, right away. Gather all the *menfolk* an' let's see if we can find out how long ago they left an' what we're gonna do about it." Slamming the screen door behind him, Peter knew he would be walking a thin line as the day unfolded.

He had put the bug in Caleb's ear the previous morning, filling him in on the community's decision about the girl's future. Not sure if the young man would actually act on her behalf, he had tried not to worry about it, either way. Now that he had, Peter Mason wasn't sure if he were glad or annoyed that his best friend's son had run off with his niece, and he certainly hoped no one discovered his part in it.

ABOUT THE AUTHOR

Anyone who knows me could tell you, I am a friendly kind of person, never met a stranger and take up conversations anywhere at any time. I work hard, and my mind never seems to shut down, as I wake up often in the middle of the night with ideas pouring out and demanding to be dealt with. Of course that means much of my books were written in the middle of the night.

I grew up and still live in the great state of Texas where everything is bigger, where we have warm weather and a central location. I love my state, my town, and my family, which includes my four sons, my significant other, and many friends as well.

I have thoroughly enjoyed writing this story and hope that you will love reading it just as much. And of course, there will be many more adventures to come.

You can follow Samantha Jacobey at:

Website: www.SamJacobey.com

Facebook: https://www.facebook.com/SamJacobey

Twitter: https://twitter.com/SamJacobey

Pinterest: http://www.pinterest.com/samanthajacobey/

41663830R00151

Made in the USA
Charleston, SC
08 May 2015